Seeing Clearly

A View from Heaven

A novel by

Rick Mapson

Seeing Clearly

by Rick Mapson

ISBN-1-442-18057-9

Printed in the United States of America

09 08 07 06 05 04 03 02

Second Printing: January 2014

Cover Design by Rick Mapson

For
Margaret the love of my life!

Acknowledgments

...

For Walter Stetter who was the first to say that Seeing Clearly read like a real novel. His help in editing and pointing out flaws was invaluable.

For Dianne Morton whose enthusiasm and belief in this project helped make Seeing Clearly a reality.

To Adam Nelson whose final edits eliminated the distractions from this story and whose encouragement was priceless.

To all of you out there who took a moment to listen and hear my heart, thank you for your encouragement and prayers.

To my children Megan, Jeff, Brad and Emily who listened to my stories and survived my battle to write.

And most of all to my Angel Margaret who believed her Dreamer could do anything (even if it took over ten years).

Message from the Author

First of all I would like to thank my Father in Heaven for taking me on this journey filled with wonder, insight, and tears. A lot of tears. Why me? I've asked that same question over and over. Actually most of the time I did the Moses thing. You've got the wrong guy and by the way, in case you haven't noticed, I can't write. Time after time I would give up and each time he would have Matthew invade my mind with his story. He didn't give up on me and I know he won't give up on you

I know there is no way I can fully show what Heaven is like. My goal is to help you to get a glimpse of our Creator and his creation without the distortion of this fallen world.

If Matthew's journey has helped you please share it with others. It has been my pleasure to share it with you. I don't know why Matthew invaded my life with his story because at the time I was not a writer. Many times I wanted to give up but I knew this was too important. If I could ask you for one thing it would be to pray that this message would reach those who need it.

Blessings,

Rick

Table of Contents

Chapter 1- Nothing
(Forty-One years ago)

"WHAT HAPPENS WHEN YOU DIE?" The words burst out of Matthew's mouth louder than he intended.

The large group was stunned for just a moment, stopping the buzz of small talk among family and friends. The words were allowed to fall to the floor as most ignored them and a few shook their heads.

Three days ago, when they told him about the death of his great aunt, the words started rolling around in his head. During the funeral service they were pushing to get out, then at the grave site "Ashes to ashes, dust to dust" seemed to push him to the brink of sanity as the coffin teetered above the hungry hole below. He hurried back to the car sure that at any moment the ground would suck the coffin into its belly and with it anyone standing too close. Now here in the large hall that had been set up with food for family and friends, the words just shot out on their own: "What happens when you die?" At nine years of age, Matthew didn't understand that a question everyone wanted to know the answer to was a question that should never be asked.

"Hey kid, way to kill the party."

Matthew turned around to see an old, rough-looking man. "I didn't mean…"

"I was just kidding. You can't kill something that's already dead."

An older lady with white hair quickly approached with her finger in the air. "Horace! Don't you bother this nice young man."

"Mabel, I ain't botherin' him, just going to help him with his question."

Mabel shook her head as Horace turned to Matthew. "What's your name, son?"

"Matthew...Matthew Peterson, sir."

"Well Matthew, I ain't no sir. I'm Horace and this here is my sister Mabel. The question you're askin' is one that makes most everyone uncomfortable. I'm not like most; I think it's good to make people uneasy, so I'm here to help. Mabel?"

Mabel pushed her lips together and out and stared at her brother. "Horace."

Horace put his arm around Matthew. "Mabel, this young man needs your help. You go to church all the time, surely you would know what happens when you die."

By now a few others had gathered around them and were all looking at Mabel to hear what she had to say.

Well," Mabel explained to those surrounding her, "The good book says if you're good you go to heaven and if you're bad you go to...you know... H - E - double toothpicks."

"You mean hell?" Horace laughed.

A well-dressed young lady approached the group. "I don't believe in hell. If there is a God, he wouldn't be that cruel."

Mabel's smile disappeared. "If there's no hell, what happened to Hitler, murderers, child-abusers and other bad people?"

The young lady's face turned red. "Maybe they just come back as a lower life form until they get it right."

"Well," Horace said, "I don't usually agree with Mabel, but if there isn't a hell, where would all the good music go? Besides that's where the party will be, not to mention all of my friends."

As Horace started to laugh, Matthew felt a large familiar hand on his shoulder. "Excuse us." Matthew's dad didn't wait for a response as he led him to the door. During the silent walk, Matthew could hear the banter of the group as it took on a life of its own. As they walked outside, Matthew could feel the cool autumn air hit his face.

"You're almost ten now."

"Next February, sir."

"Well soon, you'll become a young man and you need to know the truth."

"The truth, sir?"

"To your question, son."

"My question?"

"What happens when you die?"

"Oh yeah."

"When you die, it's the end. Ashes to ashes, dust to dust."

"But sir, what about Heaven? Grandma says Grandpa is in Heaven and if we know God we can go there too."

"Heaven is for kids and women who can't live with the truth, or people who need a crutch. Once you die, there is nothing."

"Nothing?"

Matthew's father looked out into the garden. "That's what I said. Nothing."

Chapter 2 - Acceptance
(Twenty-five years ago)

Matthew couldn't wait for the elevator choosing instead to run up the three flights of stairs, his lank six-foot, one-inch frame eating up three steps of faded orange carpet at a time. Matthew was startled as the third floor door came into view. He did not remember seeing the second. After he opened the door to his floor, he stood for a moment to steady himself and looked at the letter that would change their lives forever. The musty turquoise carpet that lined the hallway made him smile as he walked down to the fifth apartment on the left. Not much of a place, but not too bad for their first place. Matthew grabbed the warm brass knob with his hand as his heart pounded in his chest.

Matthew threw open the door to their small one room apartment, startling Jane, who had just put the cushions on their foldaway sofa bed. Closing the door behind him, he waved the letter in the air. "It came!"

Wrapping her arms around him, she rested her chin on his shoulder and breathed into his ear, "Why don't you open it?"

They both watched his index finger poke in on the side of the envelope and then slide the length of it. He pulled the letter free and opened it so they both could read:

Dear Matthew Peterson,

We are pleased to inform you ...

The rest became a blur as Matthew swung Jane around in his arms. "Yes! We made it, we're in!"

Jane could see fire in his eyes. She had seen it many times before: when he made the dean's list, when he aced a big test, and now with his acceptance into residency at Mercy Memorial. That passion and competitive spirit had drawn her to him but this time it scared her. She had only seen this intensity once before, the first time they had made love. She knew what this letter meant to him, but she wasn't sure she could compete. For that matter, she didn't know if she even had to. This letter held his future, but would it hold hers?

Jane shook off the feeling and pushed him to arm's length. Tilting her head, she said, "We?"

"Of course we!" Matthew exclaimed in surprise.

Jane tore the letter from Matthew's grasp and pushed him backward on the sofa. She gave him her stern look and tried her best not to smile. "The only 'we' I saw was someone congratulating a Matthew Peterson." She quickly glanced at the letter and then back at Matthew. "Nope, no Jane Robinson."

Matthew struggled to get up as she put her finger in his chest, pushing him back on the sofa bed. He tried to speak and she silenced him by pointing at him. "Utt!" she said.

Jane held out her hand, palm up, as if waiting for something. Matthew smiled and shook his head. Putting his hand to his lips, he "locked" his mouth by turning an imaginary key. Then he placed it in her hand. The game had begun!

She slipped the "key" into the small pocket of her tight-fitting jeans, giving him a wink. "Very good. Maybe there is a 'we,' just maybe." Then she turned around to the room and addressed it as if a jury surrounded them. She lifted up the papers, and said, "I just don't see it in these papers, do you?"

Matthew enjoyed being prosecuted by Jane. Win or lose, they would usually wind up in bed. He knew she would have made a great public defender if she hadn't given it up to help him through med-school. He also knew the fear she tried to hide. He had overheard one of her friends: *Use 'em and lose 'em, that's what they do. Before he becomes Doctor Matthew Peterson, you'll be on the street.* Instead of feeling anger, he smiled, knowing that in a moment he would vanquish that fear forever. Still sitting on the sofa behind her, Matthew frantically waved his hands.

She turned around. "What's this? The defendant wants to speak?" She turned back to the jury. "What do you say, ladies?"

With this, Matthew gave the virtual audience his best lost puppy dog face.

Jane glanced at Matthew and then back to the jury. "I don't believe you're going to fall for that." Pointing at Matthew, she said, "Conference, in my chambers!"

Matthew always liked this part, where Jane and the ladies would confer. Jane walked over to the corner of the room by the desk and looked out the window. "Wow, Tommy's out jogging again." She tilted her head to one side. "Yeah, nice buns." She glanced back at Matthew, talking just above a whisper. "You know he can't be trusted." Then she shook her head. "I know he's cute. You can't fall for that. Okay, okay we'll hear him out, but I tell you he's up to something…"

Jane turned back to a beaming Matthew. She walked over to him and slid her finger into her pocket to retrieve the key, then pointed at him. "No funny stuff, mister."

He shook his head and breathed in the White Shoulders perfume he gave her last Christmas. He couldn't help giving the make believe jury a wink as she bent down to turn the key. He stood up as she sat down and tried his best not to smile. "Ladies of the jury, I contend that the problem is not that the name is incorrect; the problem is that it's incomplete." With that, he snatched the letter from her.

"Hey!" she said, struggling to get the letter back.

"Exhibit A, remember?" he said while holding the letter away from her.

"Fine," she said. Slowly, she sat back down. "What do you mean it's not complete?"

Turning his back on Jane, he pulled the pages from the envelope and waved them in the air for effect. "I intend to prove my client is innocent." He looked over the contents as he nodded his head. Jane didn't see the pen he quickly pulled from his front pocket to jot something down on the first page.

"What are you doing?"

"Nothing," he said, turning around and stuffing the letter back in the envelope. Bending on one knee, with his eyes aflame, he handed it back to Jane.

"You nut. You switched it!"

"Never. It wasn't incorrect, just…"

"Incomplete, I know."

Matthew raised his hands. "Open it. You'll see."

"I know you're up to something, mister," she said, pointing her finger at him. She reopened the letter. Her hands started to shake as she read where he had written *Mr. & Mrs.* in front of Matthew Peterson.

Matthew stood and smiled as he drew an imaginary sword and slashed at her dragon of doubt, vanquishing it from her mind forever. He sheathed his weapon and raised his hands victoriously. Kneeling back down, he gazed into her hazel brown eyes, which were brimming with tears. "Marry me, Jane. Make an honest man of me."

"You're crazy."

"Oh yeah?" he said. He went to the small apartment's front door and clicked the lock.

"We have four weeks before I start." He turned back toward Jane. She wasn't smiling. "What's wrong?"

Jane patted the cushion next to her. "We need to talk."

Matthew started to open his mouth, but nothing came out, so he sat down next to her. Staring into space, he tried to focus on the future but all he could see was the old peeling wallpaper. He had never thought that Jane might not want... him. He always knew she was out of his league. Sure, he had come from a much more privileged slice of society, but with him came baggage, maybe too much baggage. Just like this rundown apartment. Jane, on the other hand, always lit up the room. She had broken through the wall he had built, letting life in. He sat frozen, contemplating how long it would take to repair the wall and knowing it would never be more than a patch. The hardness she had been able to break through started to crystallize on his face.

"Matthew... Matthew." His name being called out softly beckoned him back through the tunnel. She put his left hand in hers. "It's not what you think... I love you Matt."

His hand tightened as the word launched itself like a suicide jumper from his bottom lip: "But?" They both sat helpless as his question fell to the floor.

She stared down, then back up into his eyes. He had never seen this kind of hurt in her before. He wanted to comfort her but didn't know how. So he just held her hand.

Jane knew he was right—there was a "but," but it wasn't what Matthew was thinking. How could she explain that she had run out of pills the week before his birthday and didn't have enough money for the refill? How she wanted him as much as he wanted her? How she took a chance? She had debated the issue for weeks. Angry at herself… angry at him… angry at life. Why couldn't he see or feel the pain she'd been going through? She had always been there for him.

"I know something's been bothering you." Whispering, he added, "I thought this would fix it."

"Not everything can be fixed." She declared it not so much to him but the world. She peered into his eyes, empty except for the ashes, wondering if she would ever again see the fire. "I'm pregnant."

Chapter 3 - Vacation
TODAY

Dr. Matthew Peterson could hardly sleep and bolted out of bed at 5:00 a.m., almost an hour early, afraid that he would oversleep. It's not that he was the morning type. Truth be told, left to his own devices, he'd be up until 2:00 a.m. Jane did her best to encourage him to get a good night's sleep. He would try to comply by being in bed by midnight. She swore residency had made him a bionic man.

Thoughts of their upcoming four-week vacation invaded his sleep most of the night. Tomorrow, he and Jane would be returning to Europe after twenty-five years. Old memories flooded back as shattered pieces of glass, each one reflecting a piercing shard of his past. Wounds he thought had healed surprisingly stung again. This time it would be different, had to be different. He had told himself he was willing to risk losing everything if he could just recapture some of what they once had. Now on the eve of their vacation, he wasn't so sure. The only thing he knew for certain was he was lonely and couldn't live that way much longer.

He closed the door to the bathroom and turned on the light. Looking back at him from the mirror was a haggard fifty-year-old man. The last time he glanced at the clock on his dresser it showed 1:57. *Three hours, could be worse*. He ran cold water from the tap over his hands then on his face, forcing the dreams of the night back into his subconscious. He slipped into the shower and got lost in the hot pulsing flow. Set on automatic pilot, he completed his usual daily routine. As he finished tying his tie, he rubbed his cheek and smelled his breath to make sure he'd shaved and brushed his teeth. He dimmed the bathroom light before opening the bathroom door.

The light filtered soft shadows on Jane as she slept. Matthew picked up his shoes and just stood there watching her for a few moments. A nervous smile appeared on his face as he mouthed the words. "I love you. I miss… us, I just wish I knew how to..." He turned away and reset the alarm to 6:50 before heading downstairs.

Matthew liked the stillness and quiet of the morning, the only interruption being Caleb, their orange-colored cat with a tiger look. Caleb followed Matthew downstairs, weaving through his legs as they walked through the den into the kitchen.

"Caleb, it's early. Can't you wait till I get my shoes on?" Matthew said as he sat down at the kitchen table.

Matthew shook his head, listening to Caleb meow as he walked through the kitchen to the back hallway and opened the plastic container against the wall. He grabbed the cup and scooped the dried cat food as Caleb made figure-eights between his legs.

Caleb started eating as Matthew poured the dried cat food into his bowl. "You're worse than Anne."

Matthew threw the cup back into the plastic container and closed the lid, stopping for a moment to watch Caleb devour his food. "Man you're gonna miss me."

Matthew turned on the coffee maker as he passed back through the kitchen and picked up a writing pad off the small table by the phone. Sitting down at the kitchen table, he looked back through the annals of time to when he and Jane first met and smiled. *This will surprise her; it's been a long time.*

He stared into the den for a minute, then started to write the first thing that came into his head. *Roses are red.* He closed his eyes for a long moment and shook his head. *No, not roses. . . not ever again. Why… why did something like that have to pop into your head, today of all days?*

He felt all emotion drain from his face, giving him a cold, mannequin-like feeling. He glanced at the calendar that hung next to the phone. October 20th *was only three days away. In three days it will be twenty-five years.*

Just say it and move on, Matthew told himself as he looked at the words for a moment before putting the paper in his pocket. The familiar emptiness ate into his soul. While his thumb pushed hard against his forefinger, he took a deep breath and released it slowly. "Sorry." He could barely hear his own whisper as the guilt of yesterday added yet another brick to today's already unbearable load.

The aroma of freshly brewed coffee pulled his lifeless body into the kitchen.

Taking the cup, he sat down at the kitchen table. The words of Paul, his therapist, echoed through his mind. *Breathe slow and deep. Take a sip of coffee. Okay, let it go. How does the coffee taste?*

After an uncomfortable pause, Paul's voice returned. *No answer?. . . okay. Breathe slow and deep; take another sip of coffee. How does it taste?*

"Fine," Matthew whispered in a low, flat tone, and the voice in his head stopped.

He took what Paul, his therapist, called a deep, cleansing breath. *Therapy, can't live with it and can't live without it... or coffee.*

He looked down into his cup. *Not bad—almost a full cup. Paul would be proud.*

He picked up the pen and started to write.

> *Hey there you sweet young thing. Okay I'm a little out of practice and it just doesn't sound quite the same as it did over twenty-five years ago, but I bet you're surprised. Just think of me as your own personal love boat for one. I know I'm still a little dingy. Get it, love boat. . . dingy? Anyway you're probably glad you don't get these silly things every day. I Love you, Jane. You're my rock. Well I've got to go. I'll be home by three, make sure Daniel's ready. Have a great day.*

Matthew had always struggled on how to sign things. *I could just sign "Love" or "Love Ya." Naw... I could say: "I miss you"... no, she wouldn't understand. I want something that she wouldn't... I've got it!* he said to himself, almost spilling his coffee. He said the words as he wrote them down:

"God Bless, Your Man Matt."

She would never expect that from me. God and me, we just don't mix. Not that we haven't tried. But it's like my dad always said: There's just no room for God in a grown-up world.

I know, Paul—transference, Yada yada yada, Matthew told himself, remembering a session he had with his therapist. *Dad wasn't*

*right all the time anyways, but the God thing just doesn't work for me.
I blame God, and he condemns me.*

Matthew tried to block out Paul's words as "transference," but
they continued to echo in his head, reminding him of one of the
sessions with Paul.

"The God thing and 'Nam are both out of bounds, remember."

*"You brought it up." Matthew could see the Paul look. That look
of satisfaction, knowing he'd gotten Matthew to go beyond their
preset boundaries.*

*"Okay, Mister Transference. How can I have transference with
something that probably doesn't exist?"*

There was the look again. "Probably doesn't exist?"

*"Do you have to repeat everything I say? Yeah, probably doesn't
exist, except for the mindless millions that need a crutch."*

*"What about...." Paul had caught him. His eyes betrayed the
laughter he was trying to hide.*

*"Except for Jane and Daniel," Matthew cut in. "If only God
were like them. Oh, and Grams. There was one special lady."*

"What makes them special?"

*"They're real and they care. With them I might have a chance,
but with God... Never!"*

"I thought God doesn't exist?" Paul prodded.

"If he does, he doesn't care, so what's the difference?"

No response.

"Paul?" Matthew said out loud, forgetting that Paul wasn't really
there. He looked around, making sure no one had heard him talking to
himself. *What have you done to my mind? You come, invade my
thoughts, and then... poof...you're gone. At least you can't charge me
for these special visits.*

Shaking himself back to reality, Matthew wrote "Jane" on an
envelope and put the letter inside.

I've still got a little time. Why not give it another try, Matthew
told himself as he took his briefcase out of the closet. Laying it out on
the kitchen table, he started the ritual. He removed the Bible from the
briefcase, and holding it between his hands, he said, "Okay God,
here's your chance. Show me." He closed his eyes as he opened the
book and placed his finger on a page.

Matthew started reading at the place his finger found—*I Am has sent me to you.*

Just like always, what kind of nonsense was that—*I Am has sent me to you.* Matthew marked the spot to prove the point. Once in a while, he would pick the Bible up and read a passage he'd already marked. He would shake his head and put it away. If there were a God, look what a mess he created. Matthew couldn't blame God too much; he hadn't done much better. On the outside, he looked great, and after years of therapy he was able to get by. A strange thought popped into his head. In a way, he and God were alike: they both made messes others had to clean up.

Jane on the other hand did real well with the God thing. She was part of a whole family of believers. To think that in the beginning he pushed Jane into taking Daniel to church. "You want Daniel to be better than us, don't you?"

"Tell the truth." Paul's voice was soft and compassionate now.

"The truth was, I pushed her to God, but the reason wasn't for her good, or even Daniel's. I… I couldn't handle her pain. The women at church were like medicine for her. After a few months I couldn't pry her away, and Daniel went everywhere she went.

*   *   *

One day she came home with a big smile on her face. "I'm a believer!"

Matthew put down the Sunday paper he had been reading and declared, "I believe in God."

She was so excited. "So did I… kind of, but now he lives inside of me."

"Your head's not going to start spinning around spewing green slime is it?" he said, quickly ducking behind the paper.

"Wise guy, I'll prove it to you," she said, ducking into the bedroom.

"Should I get a plastic tarp?" As quickly as she disappeared, she returned with the box. The box Matthew hated to see. The life drained from his face as she approached his easy chair.

She took his paper, placed it on the floor, and sat in his lap and smiled. She opened the lid and waved her hand over the box toward him.

As the scent of rose petals filled the air, she kissed him on the forehead.

"I'm okay. For the first time in a very long time, I'm really okay." She reverently closed the lid and gave it to Matthew. "It's yours now; I'm ready to let it go."

* * *

Matthew got up and put the box in the back of the closet. Once in a while he still looked to see that it was there, but he didn't have the guts to open it. He knew someday he'd have to face it, knowing her will stated that the petals be sprinkled on her grave. "Man, I have to die first."

It had been twelve years since she let it go. How he envied her. She was at peace.

His Grandmother's words echoed through his mind. *Every new day springs eternal.*

"Maybe today, Grams, maybe today." Matthew smiled as he picked up his briefcase and headed out to the car.

Chapter 4 – Last Patient

Matthew's half-hour drive to the clinic went by quickly. Steppenwolf's "Born to be Wild" helped to trim five minutes off his commute and a few years off his life.

Get your motor running…looking for adventure…

In whatever comes our way…Gonna make it happen,

Take the world in a love embrace.

Born to be wild… We have climbed so high…

Never want to die…We were born to be Wild…

He liked to get to the office a little before the crowd to get a good parking spot. To his amazement, Walt's Beemer was parked in Matthew's usual spot. "Walt's in early; that's a first."

Matthew skipped a spot and pulled in. When he got out he admired the new BMW. "Nice, still has temp tags. Someday Matt, someday."

"Hey!"

Matthew turned in surprise and almost walked into the car. "Anne, don't do that!"

"Don't set off his alarm; you know how he is with his toys," Anne said.

Matthew joined her, and they walked together. "Why's he in so early?"

"I think he's meeting with the board tomorrow." Anne smiled. "Last minute cramming, you know, vintage Walt."

They walked across the street; Matthew scanned his ID card and opened the door for Anne. "How's the day look?"

"I tried to clear most of it, but you know how that goes," Anne said as they reached Matthew's office.

"Remember, I need to be out of here by two-thirty."

Anne started down the hall. "Don't worry; I'll push you out on time."

The morning was packed and didn't give Matthew much time to reflect on being out of the office for four weeks. The afternoon was clear for paperwork and one last-minute patient.

"Dr. Peterson, your last patient has just arrived," Anne said after a quick knock and entering his office.

Matthew looked up from behind his desk. "Thank you, Anne. I'll be with him in a minute."

With that, Anne whirled around and disappeared, the door closing behind her, leaving him alone with his thoughts.

"Last patient." Anne's words hung in the air.

You would think it was my last meal, not my last patient. Vacation… It sounded great in theory, but now that he could see it on the horizon, it terrified him. After twenty-five years they had, or at least he had, built a comfortable distance between himself and Jane. Time had done its work, and he had let it happen.

He wanted more, needed more. Where was the man he used to be—full of life instead of running on empty all the time? At romance, he was one of the best. Now his best was the fake, plastic feeling he felt the few times he tried to compete with the man he knew he once was. On the inside he was the same, except for the loneliness and doubt. Not letting anyone in had taken its toll. At this point, he wasn't sure if he *could* just relax and enjoy himself. He was always the man in control, and even if it made him nervous, he needed it that way.

He was also prone to doing something stupid. *What if four weeks were not enough? Or what if it was too much?*

Life's currents had been pulling him and Jane in different directions—she becoming more involved in her church, and he with his profession. Sure, they went on dozens of vacations with their son Daniel and a few weekend getaways themselves, but now they needed more. Or did they?

Anne opened the door and stood in the doorway with her hands on her hips. "Dr. Peterson, your patient is waiting." Then she saw the lost look in his eyes. "Is everything okay?"

Matthew rose from the chair behind his desk, trying to shake himself back into reality. "Yeah, sure… I guess I'm just a little nervous."

"It's just a little cold with a low-grade temp, nothing to worry about." Anne teased.

Matthew shook his head. "That's not what I meant and you know it. Thanks."

He smiled as he walked down the hall. Anne always knew how to get him out of a mood. He stopped outside examination room B3 and picked up the patient chart from the pocket on the door. Matthew glanced at it as he entered the small exam room where Mr. Holloway was already sitting on one end of the table.

"How are you feeling today, Mr. Holloway?"

"Doc, I just can't seem to shake this cold." He let out a muffled cough as if to prove the point.

"Well, let's have a look shall we?" Matthew said as he grabbed a tongue depressor from the jar on the counter. "Open. Mm hm, looks like you've had this cold for a while now, enlarged glands, redness, and sinusitis. You should've come in a week ago. Don't wait so long the next time, okay?"

Matthew gave Mr. Holloway his stern but concerned doctor look as he wrote out the scripts. "Here are two prescriptions. Take the antibiotic with a meal once a day and the decongestant three times a day. If you're not feeling better in a few days, come back in and see Dr. Rosen. Make sure to take all ten days' worth of antibiotic. Very important, even if you're feeling better."

"Sure Doc, thanks."

Matthew walked down the hallway and as he entered his office he felt a coldness. The office felt strange, almost like it wasn't his. Sure, all the things were his: the desk, the pictures, the degrees on the wall, even the pen and pencil set his son had given him for his fiftieth birthday earlier this year. It was like he had been gone for a long time.

He closed the door and leaned back against it, trying to gather his thoughts. He closed his eyes. A second later, he opened them to find the feeling gone.

He pushed the COM button. "Anne, can you come in?"

As Anne entered the room, Matthew locked his desk and picked up his briefcase and the small stack of papers.

"Well, I guess I really am going." He handed the papers to her. "Here's my itinerary and the numbers you wanted."

Anne walked with him down the main hall. "I'll give Jane a call to let her know you're on your way. You two have a great time."

As he reached the front door, he turned and gave Anne a hug. "Thanks for everything, Anne. Be well."

Matthew opened the large front door. The cool autumn breeze rustled the leaves and left a refreshing feeling on his face.

He took in a deep breath and let it out slowly as he took a moment to watch the leaves dance in the swirling autumn wind. He smiled to himself as he walked across the street into the covered parking garage. He was as free as the wind.

* * *

"Daniel, can you double…"

Jane's voice was drowned out by the ringing of the phone. She glanced at the caller ID and picked up the phone.

"Hi, Anne… Did you kick him out yet?… Yeah, weird. Well sometimes big events do make him spacey… Really, twilight zone, yeah…. You want 'out there'? He wrote me a little note this morning; you won't guess how he signed it… Anne, be nice… He's romantic in his own way… It wasn't that; he signed it 'God Bless.' Anne… Anne, are you there?… Yeah, should be quite the vacation… Keep praying. Maybe he needs this vacation as much as I do… Thanks, oh sure. Gotta go… Yeah last minute, you know. Gotta go. God Bless."

Daniel eyes met his mom's as she hung up the phone. "Everything okay? Is Dad zoning again?"

"Yeah, you could say that. He actually wrote me a little note. You'll never guess how he signed it."

Daniel gave his mom the teenage *you really don't want me to go there* look.

"Be nice. He signed it, 'God Bless.'"

"A lot of things ran through my mind, Mom. That for sure wasn't one of them."

Jane smiled. "Daniel, you never know."

Chapter 5 - Surprise

Matthew entered the garage and glanced at his watch—2:39 p.m., nine minutes late. "Not too bad," he told himself, quickening his pace. As his eyes adjusted to the light he saw a kid walking his way. He must have been only twelve or thirteen.

"Hey mister, got any spare change? I need some money to help my Mom".

The kid was a mess. With badly stained and tattered clothes, matted hair, and a strong odor, he would have been the perfect poster child for the disadvantaged. Matthew wondered why he wasn't in school and if the administrators were aware of his truancy. He was working at being tough, but his young face exposed his nervousness.

Matthew reached into his back pocket and smiled. As the boy smiled back, Matthew could swear the boy licked his lips.

Matthew timed it perfectly, quickly jerking his empty hand out of his pocket. "Not!" he said, starting to laugh.

Immediately the boy's expression changed, not to what Matthew expected, but to one of fear and pain. Feeling bad, Matthew quickly grabbed his wallet and fished out a few bills. "Hey, kid, it's okay. I was just having a little fun. Seriously kid, here's a little something. But to assure your future success you really need to finish school."

The kid glanced past Matthew as he put his wallet back. Matthew heard the sound of a click and felt the presence of someone behind him. Fear and panic shot through him as he tried to spin around quickly. He felt heavy and weighted down as he pushed against time, but he could barely move. His sinuses filled his head and he could no longer hear anything but the pounding of his heart.

Matthew's body was slowly turning as his mind raced. He needed to know who was behind him! He saw the image of a teenager pass into his line of sight. He was about eighteen, tall and gaunt. His eyes were dark, empty, and cold, matching his expressionless face.

Then, suddenly, the young man started to smile. It triggered a switch in Matthew, causing the last moment to flash by. He could hear and breathe. He relaxed and returned the smile. Then he saw it. He had been looking so much at the young man's face he hadn't seen it. He glanced down just in time to see the garage light reflect off the knife the young stranger held at his side. Before he could react, the assailant lunged at him. Matthew winced but didn't feel anything.

Time seemed to slow again, allowing Matthew a moment to evaluate the scene. *How could he have missed it?* He was so close now he could feel the heaviness of his assailant's breath, but where was the pain? Then he saw it. The handle of the knife was sticking out of his abdomen.

Time rushed back like a bolt of lightning as pain shot though him. He doubled over and the assailant grabbed the knife with both hands and pushed Matthew backwards. He heard the sound of his own head hitting the concrete floor. The pain was already so great he didn't even feel his head hit. He looked up as through a fog and saw the younger boy's face staring down at him. The kid was crying. "Sorry mister." The doctor blacked out as the older boy turned him over to get the wallet.

* * *

When Matthew came to, he found himself lying face down between two parked cars and staring at the tire of a BMW. He felt his head pounding. He tried to move but couldn't. This was no dream. He closed his eyes, and the whole scene replayed in his mind. He shuddered as he remembered the young boy, the older youth, his disarming smile, and the knife. As he remembered seeing the reflection of light he flinched inside, but his body wouldn't move. He started to scream, but blood flooded his mouth. The side of his head was wet and sticky. Lying there, he tried to look behind the parked car into the parking garage. He saw the trail of blood, his blood, from where they had dragged him.

He had to think! *The Beamer, try to move and touch the Beamer, just set off its alarm and you'll be ok.* His body just laid there deaf to his commands.

Okay Matt, remember your training. If you got through 'Nam you can get through this. Forget the pain. Evaluate the situation, make a plan, then execute the plan. Place—you're lying next to a car. Condition—you were stabbed and lifted off the ground and have lost a lot of blood. You fell to the ground on the back of your head and lost consciousness. How long were you out? How bad is the bleeding? Was an artery cut?"

He was still unable to move. *Did the knife reach my spine? The car, if I could just set off the car alarm.* The tire of the BMW looked so close; it couldn't have been more than a foot from him, but it began to look farther and farther away. Then he felt warmth on his fingers. It was his own blood.

You're dying, Matt. How many times have you seen it when someone was going to die? They knew they weren't going to make it. You can feel it surrounding you.

* * *

"Maggot! You can't die until I give the order, UNDERSTAND!"

"What?" Matthew asked in confusion. He looked past the car and could just make out the image of his old drill sergeant. *"Yes, sir."*

His eyes exploded. *"What?!"*

"Sir. Yes, sir. Sergeant Mack, heartless purveyor of misery."

"Pain is you friend. Pain will help you get home, son."

"I'm trying, sir. . . I feel so cold. I want to make it home, but. . . I don't know if I can."

Mack's eyes softened as he started to fade. "I know, son. I know."

Matthew tried to fight, but without the pain, he was losing the battle and with it, his grip on this world. He was okay except for the fact that he was trapped inside this body... this body that was dying. His mind was still intact, continuing to review the situation.

This icy fear began to penetrate his bones. The floor of the parking garage was wet with his blood, the blood that held his life. He wanted to look away, but he couldn't. He tried to close his eyes, but the darkness was worse. He could see the scene before him changing ever so slowly. There was a complete and utter stillness except that the bright red of his blood was changing, becoming darker and darker.

As the hallucinations faded to black and white he saw his friend Joey sitting on the garage floor watching an old TV set. He turned to look at Matt. *It's just syrup. My Uncle Tyrone says so. Looks more like blood than blood.*

It's blood alright, Joey.

Naw, how'd you know?

Because it's mine.

Oh, I guess you're right. You dyin'?

Matthew started to hear what sounded like ringing as Joey disappeared, leaving an empty garage. This last lonely scene started to move away from him as he sank into himself. As it moved away he tried to hold on to it. It was all he had left, and now it, too, was leaving. As it receded, the ringing and all the remaining sounds of life attached themselves to the picture and slowly moved away. The sound was now only a whisper.

Soon all noise was replaced with one single sound—Matthew's heart, which was, with each beat, pumping away his life. With each beat came the fear that it would be his last. His life… his life… his life. Soon to be his death. Death… he had seen enough of it, from Vietnam to the emergency room. It didn't matter—death was death. When you die they put you in a bag, THE END.

The end—I'm not ready for the end. I still have so much to do. I don't want this to be the end.

This is not fair. Wasn't I a good guy? I don't deserve to die like this. Then the anger started to boil inside him. *Why, God? Why? You say you're out there, then WHY? Aren't you supposed to know everything? Why didn't you stop this from happening? Just like always, you do nothing!*

Then everything went black. He was completely and totally alone, cold, and afraid. He felt like a rabbit caught in the mouth of his predator, waiting for the end. He knew he was screaming with all of his might, but even the voices in his head were silent. Then he stopped, like a child terrified of the dark.

Matty, you okay?

Matthew tried to look around. *Its dark, Grams. I'm scared!*

I know, dear. Sometimes it has to be dark on the outside. It's what's on the inside that counts.

But I'm afraid.

Remember, Matty, what we do when we're afraid. Let's pray. Now I lay me down to sleep. I pray the Lord my soul to keep and if I die before I wake I pray the Lord my soul to take.

I don't want to die, Grams.

No one wants to die, Matty. It's just something that will happen to all of us, dear.

I don't want it to happen to me, Grams. I'm not... He noticed she was no longer with him.

"Grams?" he whispered.

The fear felt like a cold hard wall that was growing, surrounding him. He felt that if he made a sound, something or someone would jump from the top of the wall, right out of the darkness, and devour him. He started to hear a faint voice, a familiar voice; it was the soothing and loving voice of his wife Jane, but he couldn't make out what she was saying.

Let me hear Jane's voice. If I'm just going to lie here and die, at least let me hear what she's saying. Please God, please.

Immediately the voice came closer as the invisible wall vanished. It may not have seemed like a miracle to anyone else, but to him it was everything. It was all he had left—her voice, her gentle voice. It seemed to wrap him in warmth, like a blanket.

Over and over again she was saying, *I love you, and God does, too.*

It was what she always said when he left to go to work. Her love was always so strong, so sure, but God? *How could God love me? How could anyone who has been in war and done the things I have done and seen the things I've seen be loved by God? How many times did I go to church with Jane and Daniel just to leave feeling like I had rejected God? Why would a God who I had rejected time after time accept me?* And yet. . . as her words gave him strength, he reached out to God.

God, I don't understand why you would want me. I'm cold, scared, and dying. You know all of the things I have done, but I want to see my wife and son again. I don't want to die!

I can't remember how the pastor said to pray. He said. . . he said it could be a simple prayer. He said a simple prayer is best, especially if it comes from the heart. He said it was as simple as A B C.

Come on, Dad! It was Daniel's voice. *It's as simple as ABC: Accept, Believe, and Confess.*

When Daniel was ten he was forever trying to convert him until one day Matthew got angry with him and told him to stop. That was a hard day. Matthew wasn't sure why he snapped. It was over five years ago, and Matthew still wished he could take the words back. Jane usually supported Matthew in everything he did and rarely got upset, but not that day. That day she gave him both barrels.

He could still hear her words like it was yesterday. "How dare you get angry with your son? He just wants a father that will be there. Not just some of the time, but all of the time. Do you know how he feels at church when the other kids ask where you are? And by the way, he has become quite good at making excuses for you. Telling them how you are a very busy doctor or that you're tired.

"The other day, he asked me if you would be going to heaven. I said I didn't know but told him he could pray about it. Oh, and just last week he told me, 'Mom I want Dad to go with us to Heaven.'"

Then he heard her voice, just like that day: *Matthew, are you going to Heaven?* This time he heard all the hurt, love, and concern in her voice.

All he knew was that he wasn't sure and time was running out. *I don't know, Jane! I just don't know!*

Dad. It was his son's voice again. *I want you to go to Heaven. I really want you to go to Heaven.*

I don't know if I can son.

Try, dad. Try really hard.

I will, son.

Chapter 6 – Good-bye

Matthew felt the familiar longing well up inside. He had been here before, and each time he had turned and walked away, but not this time. He no longer cared about self-sufficiency, looks, or indifference as he began to call out to God.

God, I don't know what I'm doing. All I know is you helped Jane and she said you would help me if I would ask you to. I'm asking. I need help. Problem is that you know the truth. The dark places I've gone. I...God, I can't do it anymore. I made a mess of everything. I need you. I...

That's all he could get out as a life of hurt, pain, and regret escaped in a flood of groaning. The weight he carried around every day fell off as the flood of grace washed over his soul.

For the first time, Matthew trusted God and felt His hand sweep though his soul. He didn't even have to think about what was next.

You do exist, and you care. How could I have been so blind, Matthew thought as another wave of God's presence permeated him with warmth and peace. Now he knew he had been sacrificing truth all along. He was starting on that road less traveled, following the unfamiliar path of grace, leaving the main highway of pride behind. The truth that he was a sinner both overwhelmed him and released him from the burdens of a lifetime.

Come on Matthew, keep going, say the name. You know you want to. You know you have to.

"Jesus." There, he said it. "Jesus." He said it again. "I know you died for me, taking my place, but I still don't understand why. Why you would die for me, but I..." Words weren't strong enough to hold the weight of gratitude he felt.

Then the realization hit him. *You are God, you... are... God! The real thing, not someone I could manipulate, or form into what I want you to be, but God in control. The God over everything. How many times you've tried to reach me and I walked away. Well I'm not walking now.* Matthew stopped. *I guess this is what it took. Forgive me for being such a fool.*

A verse came back into Matthew's memory. *For God so loved the... the world that he gave his only... only... only... I can't remember... be ... ah... only son that he that believes in him... will... will not perish but have ... have... everlasting LIFE! GOD I BELIEVE! I BELIEVE! PLEASE FORGIVE ME AND ACCEPT ME. I WANT TO GO TO HEAVEN!*

For years Matthew had felt the burden of tears without being able to shed a single one. For the first time since he was a child he felt hot tears flow from his eyes, washing away guilt and fear. Taking their place was a peace that he could not begin to understand. He felt God's loving hand surround him. As he wept, he could sense a cleansing taking away the pain and loneliness. The pain he was never able to share with anyone else he now shared with God. Still in the darkness, he could hear the very faint beating of his heart, but instead of fear he felt peace.

Oh God, how much time I've wasted! I didn't know. I just didn't know. I was a fool. If only I would have trusted you. God please let me live so I can do something real. Something not for me but for you.

His heart was pounding as his body took a deep breath and exhaled. All of a sudden, the darkness left as he felt his eyes blink. Matthew's eyes opened, and he could see. He could hear, and as he got up, he felt warmth all over. His legs and arms felt strong.

"God has... I can speak!" The words flowed from his mouth instead of blood. "God answered my prayer!"

Matthew danced around. "I'm alive! I'm alive!"

Then he heard a voice behind him as a hand touched his shoulder. "There is nothing you could do for God to cause him to love you any more than he always has," said the stranger, who moved to his side.

Matthew turned and saw a huge, well-built young man smiling at him. "Whooha, you must have eaten your Wheaties. Man, my wife is never going to believe this!"

At this the young man shook his head and pointed down to the ground where Matthew had been.

Matthew's heart sank; he looked at his hands. No blood. His shirt—no hole, no blood. For a brief second, he thought... but then he saw the blood on the parking garage floor heading toward the BMW. He looked up at the stranger. The stranger's face was sad now as he pointed to the car. He knew the stranger wanted him to look, but he didn't want to. He looked up as if to say, "I... I can't" and saw a tear starting to form in the corner of this young man's eye. His mouth formed the word *look*.

Matthew's eyes followed the trail of blood to the lifeless body lying near the car. As he got closer, he knelt and looked into the face that he had seen so many times in the mirror. That face had always been striving and pushing for what seemed of little importance now. "That's strange; my part is on the wrong side."

Now that face showed no sign of striving nor concern for the business that had consumed his time. The hurriedness was gone. There was a peace in that stillness. It looked as though he was about to say something. He saw the sadness in his eyes and completed the word his mouth couldn't say. "Goodbye."

"Goodbye," he said again as he touched his own face, brushing away the hair from his eyes. He looked at the stranger and whispered, "I need a haircut." Then, holding his own lifeless body, he collapsed, sobbing uncontrollably.

Matthew wept for the life he had missed, for the closeness he could have had with his wife and son. He sobbed for those he was leaving behind and for the time he no longer had. He cried just to cry.

After a while, he noticed a deep stillness as he sat there quietly holding the shell that once was Matthew Thomas Peterson. "You held on so hard to worthless things, letting the precious slip through your hands," he said as he rubbed a scar on his thumb.

He knew and remembered every bump and scrape. He was slowly saying good-bye to the only thing he knew as home. That piece of flesh had become him and held his life; now it was only a shell, an empty house.

He looked up at the young man. "I heard once that life was but a breath. I don't know if it was even that long."

He gently placed his body where it had been as if to not disturb it from sleeping. Matthew stood up next to the stranger, who was now his only companion. The parking garage started to look peculiar, like it was part of a poorly done film that was being run with another film at the same time, then another, then another. Matthew didn't know it, but time was converging on itself until all that was left was a dark gray fog that you could see but not feel.

He had no problem looking at his companion, but he couldn't see anything else. The traveler, who had obviously been this way before, pointed behind him, and as Matthew Peterson turned, he saw it—a beam of light piercing the gray darkness. When it started, it was no bigger than the head of a pin and looked like someone poked a tiny hole in the wall of gray. The hole grew, eating away the film of time.

Chapter 7 - Fire

Anne had just finished reading the note from Matthew and was going over next week's schedule when the fire alarm sounded. She opened the closet, retrieved her fire hat, and put it on. "Great, just what I need," she muttered.

Scurrying down the hall, she yelled, "Fire alarm! Everybody out the front door. We meet across the street in front of the parking garage."

Anne checked all the rooms, making sure everyone had cleared out. "Great, he's not even gone fifteen minutes. If this is one of his pranks, it'll be his last!"

She grabbed her bag on her way out. "Everyone across the street," Anne yelled above the alarm as she shepherded her flock to the front of the parking garage.

"You know it's a false alarm," said one of the older employees.

"Yeah, no smoke, no smell," added another.

"I know," answered Anne, "but Autoalarm has already called the fire department, and they would kill me if you were still inside when they came."

After a few minutes, little groups formed, talking about sports, family, and their plans for the weekend.

Martha walked over to Anne, who was looking at the building and shaking her head. "It could be worse. There could be a fire, instead of just a false alarm."

Anne turned to Martha. "I just hope they come soon."

They both stood in the awkward silence. Anne knew what Martha wanted. "Okay, make it a short day, but you owe me."

"You sure? I do have a party to get ready for tonight."

"Yes, I'm sure. I'll just suffer here alone."

"Dr. Peterson hasn't been gone a half hour and you already sound like him."

Anne felt a shiver. "Scary."

"Just don't let it happen again, young lady," Martha said in her best Dr. Peterson voice.

Anne smiled, shaking her head. "Have a great weekend, Martha."

"Thanks, you too," Martha said as she picked up her things and headed into the garage.

Chapter 8 – The Path

The light felt warm and inviting. Matthew closed his eyes but still saw the light. Then light was passing through him and with it the memories of a lifetime. All the light he reflected during his entire lifetime was now being recalled, focused back on him. He had become a light magnet. It felt warm, and in the span of a moment the memory of his entire life entered his consciousness. It wasn't like seeing his life flash before his eyes but rather like having total recall of his life. By now he and his companion were both totally enveloped by the light. They were bathed in it; as it passed into Matthew, he turned to his guardian and smiled. He didn't know why he just felt so good. This wasn't a smile-for-the-camera smile. It was a Dad-I-was-chosen-as-the-captain-of-the-football-team smile, a Mom-I-met-the-prettiest-girl smile, and a honey-we-have-a-beautiful-son smile all wrapped up into one. His companion's yes-I-know smile radiated back. Matthew never realized how much people communicate with their smiles; from the I-hate-your-guts smile to the honey-junior's-asleep smile.

"I am called Raah. I will take you to where you are to go."

Matthew stuck out his hand. "Hi, I'm Matthew."

Raah kept his hands at his side and gave a slight bow. "We are not permitted to touch at this time."

Matthew put his hand at his side and returned the bow. "When in Rome… You know, Raah, I remember everything: every date, every time, even every moment, like it's indexed, ready to be recalled. I even remember growing up in the old area of Minneapolis, playing in the abandoned houses; even the old lady, Miss Grace, who lived down on the corner. She would give us treats for trying to memorize the Bible, and if we memorized the 23rd Psalm she would give us an ice cream cone.

"I can remember when I got my ice cream cone. I was only five years old when I recited the whole thing. 'The Lord is my shepherd: I shall not want. He maketh me to lie down in the green pastures: he leadeth me beside the still waters.' I can even remember the green sweater she wore. 'He restoreth my soul. He leadeth me in the paths of righteousness for his name's sake. Yea, though I walk through the valley of the shadow of death, I will fear no evil: for thou art with me.' We met every Tuesday at 3:00 p.m. 'Thy rod and thy staff they comfort me. Thou preparest a table before me in the presence of mine enemies: thou anointest my head with oil; my cup runneth over.' Billy took three more weeks to get his cone. 'Surely goodness and mercy shall follow me all the days of my life: I will dwell in the house of the Lord forever.' Forever, I guess that is what this is." Life seemed so short.

"I can think of any event in my life and remember more than I could when it happened. I was the pitcher for the third grade against the fourth grade. I can remember every pitch.

"We moved eight times—my father traveled the fast track in business. What's amazing is one year we made a trip across the United States and recorded the states off the car's license plates...Now I remember each license number!

"I was always terrible at remembering names, but now I can remember every name I ever heard.

"For some reason I can remember how many times we played football on Cherrywood Drive right after we got off the school bus. I remember how many times I was quarterback, end, blocker, even how many passes I threw.

"I can't believe how much I had forgotten." He paused for a moment, then laughed as something else came to him: "Paul McCartney—'Just a Silly Little Love Song.'"

"What's that?" Raah asked.

"That was our song. She was wearing a white tank top with yellow on the edges, tight-fitting jeans...Jane...Oh Jane, I miss you already. I wanted to grow old with you."

Then Daniel came to mind: "Daniel, there's so much I wish I could do with you. I can't wait to see you again."

After a long pause, Raah smiled, "You will, Matthew, you will."

Once the light completed its work, Matthew found himself walking on a small path, which seemed to be cut out of the side of the mountain. Everything looked so clear—no gray here! To his left was a wall of solid rock, and to his right was the edge of a cliff. The path was about ten feet wide and covered with grass that was short and full like the fifth fairway at his dad's country club. As they walked up the path, another trail came into view across the chasm. The further up they went, the closer it was. He could see there were people walking down the other side.

Before long, the other path was only thirty feet away. It was close enough to see that the people walking down the other side were all crippled. They had withered arms, legs, faces, and disfigured bodies. Matthew was disturbed and shocked. Their bodies were bad enough, but the sounds they made were hideous. Through the screeching and moaning he could feel their anger, bitterness, and pain, sounding eerily haunting across the divide. They started to yell and curse at him.

One man with a limp and a deformed mouth turned and glared at Matthew from across the chasm. "What are you looking at?" he snarled.

Another one stopped. "You think you're better than us. Just wait—you'll get yours. Don't you know God hates you?"

Others stopped and added to the yelling, forming a small crowd.

"Just wait, you'll get yours!" one said, echoing the others.

"Don't you know? God hates you!" spewed another.

Then others joined in: "God hates you!" "God hates you!" "God hates you!" "You'll get yours!" "You'll get yours!" "LIAR!" "You've lied like us!" "You've cheated like us!" "You're no better than us!"

A tall, badly deformed man tried to throw something at him with his withered hand. "Hey, stop looking at us. You're a sinner just like us."

Then they started to chant. "Liar…Cheater…Liar…Cheater."

None of them would help each other, but their hatred of Matthew seemed to draw them together for a brief moment. Most of them were so angry it was impossible to make out their obscenities. Matthew hurried up the path, away from their chants and their pain.

Even as the distance between them grew, their words and sounds seemed to follow, chilling his spirit with pain, fear, and suffering that wouldn't let him go. This was very troubling after experiencing God's warmth and peace. He struggled to hold tightly to the peace, trying not to allow the evil to disturb him. *God hates you. You're a fool. You'll get yours.* He knew he deserved to get his, but he also knew God loved him even if he didn't understand why. *What did they mean? I'll get my what?* And why were they so upset with him? Some of them were so deformed they were crawling, but they were all so angry that none of them would help each other. If only he could help, but the abyss was too wide between them. He got the feeling that none of them wanted help. Their anger was so great that all they wanted to do was strike out at everyone else.

As the gulf widened and the sounds in his head faded, he started to talk to Raah. "I thought when crippled people died they would no longer be crippled. Why were those people so deformed and full of hate for God?"

Raah's face was full of compassion and sadness as he spoke. "Remember your body, what happened to it?" he asked. "And where is it now?"

"I was stabbed, but now I feel great. No pain at all." Matthew patted his stomach.

Raah raised his eyebrow. "Then what is still lying on the garage floor?"

"My body," Matthew said, thinking. "Wait a minute, if my body is still lying on the floor of the garage, then what is this?" He motioned to himself.

Raah replied, "When you die, your body is left behind. What is left is your soul. All the things you did in life affected your soul."

Matthew began to ponder two things. One from his companion— *all the things you did in life affected your soul*—and the other from those full of anger and hatred—*just wait; you'll get yours*.

Now being able to remember everything that had happened in his life wasn't such a great thing. In life he didn't consider himself a thief, but his own memory disputed this. He used to shoplift with his friends. A few times he took things from his parents and friends. He remembered stealing things, many things; from his brothers, his sisters, parents, friends, school, stores, work. The list seemed to go on and on. In each one he had an excuse, and most of the time Matthew didn't get caught.

Matthew was always able to justify everything he did, but now his life was before him and the truth of his life in the face of eternity could not be denied. He had done everything for his own benefit.

He always took shortcuts. Sometimes it meant cheating. Other times it meant just not telling the truth. The truth was always just something to be manipulated, until now. And what about the lust: lust for things, lust for his job, for power, and of course, for women? Oh sure, he was faithful to his wife. He never touched another woman, but he did a lot of looking and dreaming. Sometimes he made plans, but he never carried them out.

Sure, they weren't major crimes. A stolen cookie here, a box of candies there. Would that cripple his soul any less? He lied time after time to cover up the stealing. Sometimes he lied to make life easier or to make the story sound better than the next guy. He even prided himself on how well he could slice up the truth or dissect it so he could cover up and deceive.

Would his soul be damned because he never desired truth? Sometimes his anger would flare up and he would go too far and hurt others with his fists or words. Words… Words of hate just like the ones that were hurled at him a few moments ago. Would he become like one of them, so bitter and torn?

Matthew decided that remembering everything in his life was a bad thing. He wondered if those angry voices were right. The one thing he knew they were wrong about was God. God loved him. He didn't know why, but he was sure that He did. If Matthew was to become crippled, it would be his own doing.

Until this point, Matthew hadn't been watching where he was going. He was just following the path. He hadn't noticed the gate.

"I CONDEMN HIM!" shouted a booming voice.

Chapter 9 - Martha

Martha was in a hurry to leave before the fire engine blocked the entrance. In her rush, she almost slipped in a small puddle of oil.

Great, I better wipe it off right away or the oil will ruin my shoes. So much for trying to hurry.

She fumbled though her purse for some tissues as she approached her Volvo, then hastily opened the door and threw her purse and bag into the passenger seat. Then she began cleaning her shoes. Martha quickly wiped her right shoe and grabbed a small plastic bag she kept under the driver's seat for such an occasion.

After placing the dirty tissue in the bag, Martha started on her other shoe. When she noticed the red smear inside the bag, she screamed, "No!" and dropped the bag. "Calm down Nebe," she said, using her father's childhood pet name for her, "it's probably just transmission fluid." She quickly checked her shoe and got into the car.

You can't just leave that there. She grabbed another bag and opened the door.

"Just pretend it's one of Cocoa's little messes," she told herself as she inverted the bag, quickly snatched up the other plastic bag and tissue, folded it in on itself, and tied it shut.

She tried not to look, but she couldn't help it. Her mouth formed the word she didn't want to say—*blood*. She was just about to start looking around, but instead jumped back into her car, slamming the door. *Wounded animals aren't very friendly, but I can't just leave. I'll drive out slowly and look. That way I'm safe, and at least I will have tried.*

Just as she started to back out, the screaming fire engine shot through the parking lot as it approached the intersection, honking so cars would clear a path.

Martha's foot slipped on the gas, causing the Volvo to lurch out of the stall. Instantly her foot slammed on the brakes; she just missed the car behind her. Now her hands were shaking and she was feeling a little nauseous. *Why didn't you just stay? No, you had to leave early so you could take it easy and have a little extra time before the party. Now look at you. What a mess. Just take a deep breath, Nebe. There's no rush now—the fire trucks are already here.*

Chapter 10 – Too Late

Startled, Matthew looked up and saw a fierce man standing next to a gate, glaring straight at him. He looked like a combination of Goliath, Genghis Khan, and Attila the Hun. Matthew cowered as the man continued.

"His own life condemns him and he knows it. The sin in his life demands DEATH!" he growled.

Matthew looked at him and felt total and complete evil. This terrifying creature looked as though he wanted to tear Matthew limb from limb and devour him.

Matthew didn't know what to do. He stood there frozen as a small hideous creature jumped from the man's side onto Matthew's head and back. He grabbed at the creature, but it was too late. This thing had already wrapped his arms around Matthew's face and neck. Fear embraced Matthew's being, consuming and paralyzing him. Fear from his entire life, including the fear he had when he was about to die, had been released to torment and destroy him.

It grew black, and he was a child again, afraid of the dark. As the gloom cleared he found himself alone in an elevator, which was in a free fall. Just before it was going to hit bottom, the scene changed and he found himself in the dark covered in sweat. Even the fears from dreams he had during his lifetime were attacking him. A blinding light was coming closer and closer. He could feel the rumble under his feet, and then came the ear-splitting blast from the train's horn. He looked down and saw he was standing on train tracks. Matthew jumped off the tracks just as the train went by.

Now he was rolling down a hill in a fog, and as he rolled, the fog started to lift. He could see he was rolling toward the edge of a cliff.

He tried to stop, but the incline was too great. He grabbed at anything and everything and finally found a small shrub with his left hand just as he started to fall off the edge. He grabbed the shrub with both hands and started to pull himself up. A snake sprang out from under the small plant, lunging toward his neck. He tried to grab the snake, but it was too late. It had already attached itself to his neck, and now both were falling into the chasm. He finally pulled the snake loose, but he was still falling into the black hole. The faint light from above grew dimmer and dimmer.

He reached out into the darkness that surrounded him and felt small twigs, which broke at his grasp. He felt like he was falling through the small branches of a large tree. He kept groping with his hands and hooked his arm around a thick rope. Somehow it stopped his fall. Matthew hung there, holding on with everything he had. The rope started to shake, and he heard a loud laugh coming from above him. As he looked up, the darkness faded and he saw the fierce face of the huge man who had condemned him. Matthew was hanging on a rope that he was using as a belt. He immediately let go of the rope and fell to the ground. He got up and tried to run, but another small creature sprang from the man's side, jumped on Matthew's back, and dug its sharp nails into his side.

Matthew only made it three steps when the feeling of hopelessness overwhelmed him. The angry voices continued to taunt him. "God hates you…Just wait, you'll get yours." Their voices wouldn't let him go. He covered his ears, but the jeers kept ringing in his head. Every memory haunted him now. Good or bad, each scene of his life was replayed. Then without warning, everyone stopped and turned toward him. Shaking their heads, they said, "Too late."

He was back at home having dinner with his family. Then suddenly, they stopped and looked at him and said, "Too late." The scene changed; he was in his sixth grade classroom. Everyone, including his teacher, stopped and turned toward him and said, "Too late." Now he was in Vietnam in the middle of a battle: All the men, both the enemy and his brothers-in-arms, stopped and turned toward him. "Too late." The scenes came faster and faster, but all ended the same. "Too late. TOO LATE. **TOO LATE!**" There was nothing he could do as he felt himself drowning.

Then he heard it, the sound of metal sliding against metal, like the drawing of a large sword. As he looked up, he saw Raah, his companion, his guide, his friend. His robe was white now, growing brighter and brighter each moment.

Raah raised his sword above his head. Matthew could see a smile on his companion's face and a tear in his eye. It was the smile of a friend, a friend full of compassion and love. The tear was a tear of joy, and Raah had a twinkle in his eye.

Matthew didn't completely understand why Raah was so happy. All he knew was that he had to trust his new friend. Raah's robe glowed white. He took a step forward and started to swing his sword toward Matthew. The blow would surely slice Matthew in two.

"Trust him, Matthew," came a voice from inside as Matthew braced for the blow.

Chapter 11 - Blood

Martha took the car out of park and started forward. "Just look ahead and drive, Nebe."

As she turned to go down the next level, she slowed. *What about the poor animal? It probably ran off, if not it's too late to be of any help anyway.*

She followed the bend to the lower level of the parking garage. *So far, so good.*

Then she saw it: a puddle of blood trailing off to the left. She started to cry. *Poor thing, I'm sure there's no helping you now. Don't look, Nebe, it will just upset you more than you already are.*

She took another deep breath and started to speed up. "Don't look!" she commanded herself, but as she drove by, she saw the side of Doctor Peterson's face lying in a pool of blood sticking out just past the back tire of a BMW. Without thinking she slammed on her brakes and hit her horn.

Anne was talking to Fire Chief Cooper while his men checked the building. They both turned when they heard the horn. Anne recognized it. "That's Martha, one of our employees. Probably hit her panic button by mistake. Are you certain a Dr. Matthew Peterson didn't set up a little surprise fire drill for us today?"

"I'm sure…." The words weren't even out of Chief Cooper's mouth when they saw Martha running out of the garage.

"Blood, there's blood in the…." She just made it to the grass before her stomach erupted.

Anne ran to Martha's side. She fumbled in her purse and grabbed a handful of tissues. She waited for Martha to finish, then put a hand on her shoulder and offered her the tissues. "Here, take these."

Martha pushed her away and pointed into the garage. "Man hurt, bloo…." She bent over and vomited again.

"I got it. You stay with her," Chief Cooper said and rushed toward the parking garage.

He headed toward the sound of Martha's car, and as he turned the first corner he saw the trail of blood and knew it wasn't good.

"Unit One, I need you in the garage now. Man down. High loss of blood, possible stabbing."

Chief Cooper quickly flipped the switch for Comm Central as he walked toward Matthew. "Dispatch… This is Station 16 Unit One. I need Sky One now."

"Rodger that. I will contact and feed your GPS location for ETA."

"Rodger," Chief Cooper said, then snapped the small radio to his jacket pocket. He bent down and tried to feel Matthew's pulse. He could hear his men running into the garage. Just as he started to feel a faint pulse, his radio came to life.

Chief Cooper, this is Sky One. We are in your area. ETA is 5 minutes. Repeat 5 minutes. Rodger."

"Faint pulse," Chief Cooper said as the paramedics arrived. They immediately took over and started cutting open his shirt to find the source of the bleeding.

"Sky One, am I glad to hear you're close," Chief Cooper said as he headed outside. "We are setting up a landing site directly south of the parking garage entrance. Lines are underground. We will mark with blue and red. Rodger."

"Great, chief, what are we looking at? Over."

"One man, fifties. Loss of a lot of blood. Possible stabbing. Unit One paramedics are with him now. Will patch you through. Rodger."

"Unit One, this is Sky One. We are on approach."

"Sky One, we have one stab wound. Possible punctured lung, head and back trauma. Have IV started, transporting to backboard. He's on the board. We're losing him!"

"We are in sight of the parking garage, see you in two."

Chapter 12 – He is Mine

Just before the sword sliced through him, he heard Raah's rich, strong voice belt out words of life. "For God has not given us a spirit of fear, but of power and of love and of a sound mind. There is no fear in love; but perfect love casts out all fear."

Matthew winced as the sword sliced through him. He heard a squeal of pain, but it didn't come from him. It came from the small creatures, which were barely clinging to him now. He could feel them loosen their grip as he felt Raah's words completing the surgery on his soul and restoring him with warmth and peace.

Raah raised his sword for another blow. Now he understood the tear of joy. Matthew could hardly handle the excitement as he smiled back at his surgeon.

Yes! Raah, Yes! His guardian's robe became so bright he could barely stand to look at him.

Raah swung his mighty sword, declaring, "For God so *loved* the world he gave his only begotten Son, that whosoever believeth in him should not perish, but have everlasting life. For God sent not his Son into the world to condemn the world: but that the world through him might be saved."

Those words shot through Matthew and vibrated throughout his entire being. He never remembered the Word of God, or any words for that matter, having so much power. He could almost taste their sweetness. The creatures fell to the ground, and all fear, hopelessness, and despair evaporated. Matthew was humbled by the strength of the love, peace, and joy that now engulfed him.

Raah, this warrior of the word, pointed his sword at Matthew and touched the tip of it to Matthew's mouth. It tasted like honey. The guardian then handed Matthew the sword and looked to the Accuser.

"His own life still condemns him and he knows it," growled the Accuser. "The sin in his life demands DEATH!"

Matthew's arms shook as he held onto the great sword. He turned to face his accuser. Now that the fear and hopelessness had left Matthew, this giant beast of a man seemed hollow. Suddenly he noticed what looked like hundreds of spider webs connecting him to this Devil. The sword in his hands now seemed alive. It shot above his head, and Matthew could feel a powerful burning deep within him. As the sword shot up it started to make a circular motion, ripping through the web as words of fire came out of his mouth. Not just any words, but powerful words—words that separate darkness and light, words that bring the dead back to life.

He could hear his own voice ringing them out for all eternity to hear. "FOR THE WAGES OF SIN IS DEATH: BUT THE GIFT OF GOD IS ETERNAL LIFE THROUGH JESUS CHRIST OUR LORD."

Matthew was shaking, the sword now at his side. The gates of heaven opened and Matthew heard the most beautiful sound he would ever hear.

"HE IS MINE!"

At hearing this, Matthew Peterson didn't wait. He ran through the Gate and down the road beyond.

Chapter 13 – Sky One

Just as Sky One touched down two paramedics shot out the back door and followed Chief Cooper into the garage. Their eyes adjusted to the shade of the garage as they turned the corner toward Matthew. Some of the firefighters had set up portable lights and moved Martha's car. Matthew was now on a backboard in the middle of the garage floor. The crash cart was open with the paddles out, but Bob, one of the paramedics, was busy applying CPR while the other, Hector, was working at stopping the bleeding. Hector was clearly the one in charge.

"Time!" Hector barked.

The fireman next to the light responded, "One minute, ten seconds."

"Give it to me on every 30-second mark."

"Rodger."

Hector looked up at the Sky One paramedics James and Lisa, running his way. "We lost him but have to stop this bleeding first."

The Sky One medic was instantly at Hector's side. "I'm James. Clamp or spreader?"

Hector nodded. "Hector. I need a spreader and light."

The voice-activated light attached to James's headgear immediately illuminated Matthew as James grabbed the spreader from the instruments Hector had laid out next to Matthew. He noticed Hector's surprised expression as he inserted the spreader. "The light's voice activated."

James's partner grabbed the air bag and nodded to Bob. "Lisa," she said.

Bob was still counting to himself as he pumped Matthew's chest. When he completed the cycle, glanced up. "Bob, welcome to the party."

Lisa smiled. "Thanks for the invitation".

"One minute, thirty."

Hector said, "Nice, a little to the right. Missed the stomach but sliced through the lower left rib and went deep. I still can't see the bleeder."

James grabbed the suction tube and started to clear out the wound.

"I see it. Artery's nicked. Clamp."

Hector didn't look away but just held out his hand. He felt the steel in his hand and grasped it. He put it into the opening, clamped the bleeder, and gently pulled it toward the surface.

"You've got six to eight centimeters," James said as he opened the suture kit with his mouth. "You ever sew one of these?"

"No. We don't have authority."

"Two minutes."

"Just hold it there. Perfect. Memorial, do we have authorization?"

The speaker on James's comm badge came to life. "This is Doctor Allison. Try the slip tube, size Red three."

James didn't hesitate. He put the suture kit down, reached into one of his many vest pockets, and pulled out two small red plastic bags. He ripped one open as the other dropped to the ground. It contained what looked like a small tube with ridges and a holder at one end. He grabbed the holder with another clamp.

"Zoom… stop," James said as he squeezed the tube through the opening in the artery.

Hector looked up to see the voice-activated magnifying glasses attached to James's headgear. "Amazing." He saw Chief Cooper looking on. "Chief, take the air bag from Lisa. Lisa, get the crash unit ready."

James started to twist the clamp back and forth. It worked like a jack to force the short end into the artery until the holder was in the middle. "Almost there."

"Two minutes, thirty."

Lisa grabbed the unit and turned on the switch. "Three hundred?"

Hector looked up at Lisa. "We may only have one shot," he said. "Let's try three-fifty".

"Three-fifty it is".

"Three minutes."

James had what looked like a small pliers in his hand and slid what looked like a mini c-clamp on one end of the pliers. He clicked a clamp on one side of the tube.

"Give me ten seconds," he said as he started to repeat the process on the other side.

"Three-fifty," Hector said as Lisa dialed it in.

She applied the gel to the paddles and waited.

James clicked the last clamp on the other side of the tube. "Done."

Hector removed the clamp from the artery and saw both sides of the artery expand around the tube. "Go!"

James quickly removed the clamp on the tube and backed away.

"Three minutes, thirty."

Lisa punched the button on the unit. "Two hundred, three hundred."

"Wait!"

Chapter 14 – Nature's Symphony

He was now in Heaven, but he wanted to get as far away from the gate as possible. As he ran, he noticed a small path off the side of the main road and took it—away from the evil, away from the pain, away from the stealing, the lies, and the anger. He was also running toward something better than he could ever imagine.

He never knew he could run like this, so fast and so far. He heard that runners could get into a zone where they don't even feel like they are running; everything just flows. He was in that zone and he was flowing as mile after mile was fed under his feet. There were many trees now. The sound of rustling leaves high in the treetops grew louder and louder as he finally slowed. Curiously, it started to sound like clapping, and Matthew imagined a huge crowd standing to their feet at the finish line. He raised his hands and the sound exploded, and as if on cue, a large flock of doves came from nowhere and flew past him high into the sky.

Matthew slowly started to walk. Then he took off again, running so fast that he had barely noticed the streets were really made of gold. So this was Heaven! Incredible beauty surrounded him, but in appearance it didn't seem much different to look at than an earthly countryside. The difference was how he felt about this place. It was peaceful and serene.

The gold under his feet beckoned him, and he touched it and it was both cool and warm. It was soft enough that when he pressed hard with his thumb it left an indented print. He looked around and saw no one. *Go ahead, Matt, no one's around*, he said to himself as he crouched low. In no time he was sitting, then lying down, looking side to side at his soft golden reflection.

He closed his eyes and started to hear nature's harmony. He could hear a small brook beyond the path in the meadow mixed with the sound of the leaves in the trees. He felt coolness from the path and warmth from the light as the sounds of nature rocked him with waves of melody.

Suddenly he had a vision. At least that's what he thought it was. As he was lying there with his eyes closed, it seemed like his eyes opened on their own, and he suddenly was flying! He was suspended up above the path, soaring just below the treetops. It happened so fast that he didn't know if he was flying or just suspended in thin air. It startled him so much that he did open his eyes. Instantly, the vision vanished and he was lying on his back on the path, looking up at trees on one side and a meadow on the other.

He got up and looked over his shoulder. He felt his back with his hands. "Nope, no wings".

He chuckled at himself. "Wings?" He checked again; he just couldn't help it. He chuckled again; one thing was for sure—vision or not, it was certainly an awesome experience.

He started to walk down the path, and nature seemed to respond to every move he made. He took a few steps and he could hear the trees, leaves, and other sounds. He stopped, and the sound stopped. He started, and the sound started.

At first he thought that nature was playing tricks on him, but as he experimented he realized that nature was just waiting for him to make music. He raised his hands quickly and he could hear and feel the roll of thunder. When he made smooth soft movements he could hear the brook mixing with a gentle breeze. With little sharp movements with his fingers he could hear the crickets responding to him.

He tried out movement after movement, hearing different types of birds and animals joining with the earth, water, and trees. He found out that if he started at his knees, began to spin as he stood up, then came back down like he just got a strike in bowling, the ground would rumble and a big fish would jump out of the stream and make a huge belly-flop!

Then it hit him: he was both the composer and the director. He had never played an instrument; he had tried, but he never stuck with it. He had always loved music, however. He had always thought that everyone, given the chance, would like to direct a symphony. Now was his chance. He started soft and light and let the momentum build. Then he started to smell the environment around him. The more powerful the music, the stronger the scent became. He could simultaneously discern each and every scent as well as the bouquet the scents made together. At times the scent was so strong he could taste it, and both the smells and the tastes reminded him of different kinds of flowers and fruit he had known.

First he conducted with his eyes closed, letting the music resonate in his mind. Then he kept them open, being drawn into his surroundings. This was the sound of life—pure, clean, joyous life. He felt a freedom he had never known before. The water, wind, and earth joined with the trees, flowers, birds, and animals to complete the symphony. Powerful, tender, precious life.

He didn't think about time. For all he knew, he might have spent a lifetime there. Just his freedom from time seemed to encourage the symphony to continue as the sounds and scents gently drifted through the trees.

Everything seemed so alive and so clear. He could feel the sounds with every part of his being. He looked at the goose bumps on his arm that reflected his enjoyment at being part of the choirs as he breathed in and tasted watermelon. He heard bees and tasted honey. It was like his whole life had been lived in a fog and now for the first time he could see clearly. His senses, which in life had been clogged, were now open and clear, allowing him to feel things he had never been able to experience before.

He hadn't noticed that he had traveled quite a ways down the path. As the last note of his symphony lingered in his ear, he just stood there with his eyes closed. Even the silence was inviting, causing him to smile as peace embraced his soul. When he opened his eyes, he saw a house in the distance.

Chapter 15 – He's Back

"Wait!" James shouted, and everyone's attention turned toward him. "The backboard is setting in his blood."

"Good catch," Hector said.

He then motioned to the firemen that had already brought Sky One's transportation gurney into the garage. "Over here!"

"On standby," Lisa said as she pushed the standby button.

* * *

Outside, Martha had just rinsed her mouth out with a bottle of water. She couldn't remember the name of the girl who had given it to her. Gina, maybe, the new intern. "Did I hear they lost him?' she said to no one in particular.

Anne finished setting up one of the portable chairs she had gotten from the firemen. "Here you go Martha."

Martha walked over to Anne and grabbed one side of the chair as Anne helped her ease down into the seat. She slowly looked up at Anne. "Is he gone?"

Anne knelt in front of Martha. "No, of course not, but in times like these I like to pray."

Martha gazed into Anne's eyes through the tears in hers. "Please do. "

Anne's looked up into the sky. "Father…" She paused as words tried to form in her mouth. "Father… Please help Matthew. Touch his body; help the paramedics to bring him back to us."

* * *

The firemen, Hector, and James lifted Matthew, backboard and all, onto the gurney as Bob and the chief continued applying CPR.

James clicked the handrail to the down position.

"Four minutes."

"Damn," Hector cursed and looked at Lisa. "Go."

Lisa clicked the blinking reset button and watched the flashing number screen. "Three hundred…"

Bob and Chief Cooper backed away.

Lisa placed the pads on Matthew's chest. "Three-fifty. Clear!"

Just a split-second later she pressed the button on the top pad with her thumb and held on tight. Matthew's body jumped as the voltage tried to restart his heart.

James was watching the tube to see if it would hold when a flood of blood filled the artery. He lost sight of it just a second when the body bounced. Silence filled the garage as he watched the blood the heart was forced to expel flow through his patch job. "Keep going… come on… keep coming. Yes."

Hector barked out "Time!" as he took Matthew's pulse.

"Four minutes, eighteen seconds!" the young fireman marking time barked back.

For the first time Hector smiled. "He's back. Steady and strong."

The garage erupted with cheers and high fives.

* * *

Anne had finished her prayer as silence seemed to surround the ladies. It was suddenly shattered when a commotion came from inside the garage and a fireman came running out. "He's back, steady and strong."

The growing crowd cheered as Anne stood up and gave Martha a hug. "You saved him, Martha. You saved him."

The response was not what Anne expected. With all of her reserves spent, Martha began to cry. "What if…"

Anne pulled back slightly. "What if? What ifs are for those of us who don't act and regret it. Not for when we do and just thank the Lord we did."

Anne stood up. "You should feel good about what you did."

Martha looked down and saw the blood on her shoe, and fresh tears welled up.

"Why are you crying now?"

"I was afraid. I was really afraid."

Anne bent over with her head next to Martha's. "You go ahead and cry. Being scared like that deserves some tears."

"Here they come," someone said as the crowd parted.

Anne knelt with her arm around Martha and cried as the firemen whisked Matthew out of the garage and into the helicopter.

She stood up again and squeezed Martha's shoulder. "I've got to make a call."

Chapter 16 – Welcome Home

It was a country-style house complete with a full wrap-around porch. His grandparents had a porch just like this one, with a swing hanging from the rafters. He remembered the times he would visit them and sit on the swing next to Grams. Most of his time was spent on the porch swing just letting his mind wander.

He went up the steps and stood on the porch, which overlooked the land.

"Beautiful, isn't it?" asked a voice from behind him.

As he turned he saw a man standing in the doorway who looked like he was in his early thirties. He wore a plain white T-shirt, jeans, and a carpenter's belt with a hammer hanging from one side. He smiled what looked like a welcome-home smile. Matthew smiled back, confused.

"How do you like it?" the carpenter asked.

"Oh, it's great. I especially like the porch; my Grams had one just like it. You have a beautiful home."

He looked Matthew right in the eye, savoring every moment. "It's not my home; it's for Matthew Peterson."

Shock, surprise, and joy hit Matthew all at once. "That can't be. *I'm* Matthew Peterson!"

"Welcome home, Matthew." The carpenter's words wrapped around him like a blanket. "I think you'll like it."

Home. Matthew mouthed the word he couldn't speak.

Home—the word always seemed to elude him. It always seemed to be the place he was leaving, not going to, or enjoying. He never had the peace he had now, and "home" now reached right down to the foundations of who he was. He looked at the house. He was overwhelmed. How could this be? His dream house before him—he was amazed at how perfect it was. Although he had never put into words all of this…it was absolutely complete.

He ran his hand along the woodwork and stared into the meadows. *I don't understand. I didn't live for God my whole life and as I'm dying, just because I ask, he forgives me. After all that I have done, God not only lets me enter heaven but also has a house built for me. Not just any house. He builds me the perfect home.*

He turned to the carpenter. "Why? Why would God do this for me when what I really deserve is to be with the walking wounded heading into hell?" Matthew sat down on the porch stairs with his head in his hands.

The carpenter put his hand on Matthew's shoulders. "When we come to the end of our understanding, we can start the adventure of knowing him."

He began to hear the sound of a young child crying. It was very faint and sounded far away. As he opened his eyes, he noticed that he wasn't sitting on the porch step but on the last pew at the church his wife and son went to. The crying was more like gentle sobbing.

Chapter 17 – The Call

"Daniel!"

"Yes Mom." Daniel walked into the room with his list. "Yes, I checked it twice. I'll be fine."

"I just want to make sure you…"

The phone rang, drowning out Jane's voice. Daniel picked up the wireless and waited for the second ring. *Saved by the bell!* he thought. "I'll be fine, Mom. Hello… yeah, she's right here. It's for you."

Jane took the receiver, "Hello… yes this is Mrs. Matthew Peterson … What?… No, he was just on his …" She went pale, steadying herself against the wall.

Daniel saw the look in her eyes. "Mom?" Daniel said, shaking his head.

Jane put her hand over the receiver. "Dad's been in an accident," she said quickly, then took her hand off the receiver and motioned Daniel to her side.

Her arm was comforting, but her words were not. "May I speak with Matthew…Oh God no… Heliported to Memorial… No I can drive. My son's with me… No, I can drive. I'm okay it's just we were… I was just… I'm on my way!"

Chapter 18 – No Other Way

They were in a church now. The carpenter was with him. He stepped into the aisle and motioned for Matthew to come with him to the front. He started to follow and felt someone pass him in the aisle, but the only person he saw in the aisle was the carpenter. He looked around; the church appeared empty. They slowly headed toward the front. When they got next to the front row, Matthew looked around, and suddenly a woman in her early forties was standing next to him.

"I'm sorry. I didn't see you," Matthew said, giving the carpenter a puzzled look.

"It's okay, Matthew—Carreen gets that a lot. Carreen, Matthew. Matthew, Carreen."

Carreen's whole face smiled back at Matthew. Matthew looked at Carreen, then back at the carpenter. "Are you guys related?"

The carpenter put his arm around Carreen. "I guess you could say that, but in a way aren't we all related?"

Then Matthew heard it again—the crying of a young child. Carreen turned and headed toward the front where a young child was kneeling at a bench with a railing. She faced the young boy and placed her hands on each side of his head. The carpenter was now right behind the boy with his hand on his back. Matthew could hear the child call out between sobs.

Matthew tried but couldn't make out what was being said, so he very quietly approached the front. Now the carpenter was kneeling with his arms around the young boy. At first Matthew thought, *Daniel*, but Daniel was much bigger than this child. This child looked about nine or ten, and Daniel was now fifteen.

As he passed the front row, he heard, "My Dad's a good man, God." The voice sounded familiar. "He's really important; he's a doctor." Matthew fell to his knees as his son continued to pray for him. "God save my Daddy. I want him, me, and Mommy to go to heaven someday." Daniel started to sob again, this time joined by the sobs of his father.

Matthew tried to control his sobbing enough to walk around the front of the altar and look at his son. He knelt down beside Carreen, facing him. "Daniel, it's me, son. I'm here."

Daniel didn't even stop to look up, but instead his sobs turned to pleadings. "God save my Dad. Please God save my Dad! I want him to know you like I know you. I think he thinks you're mean, but I know you're not. If he would just get to know you, then he would understand." Carreen gently stroked Daniel's hair as his voice started to change from despair to hope.

Matthew could only sit there gazing into his son's face as he continued his talk with God. "My Mommy knows you real good and she wants Daddy to know you too. That's two of us, and Mommy said if two of us pray that God counts it as a whole lot. God, I can tell my Daddy is sad inside a lot. I think it is because you're not there to cheer him up. You could cheer him up just like you cheer me up when the school and church kids pick on me. Except for Tommy—he's real nice and makes me laugh. Did you teach Tommy to laugh? I bet you did. You could teach my Daddy to laugh when his past makes him sad. Mom says sometimes the past makes my Dad feel really sad. Please God, save my Dad."

"Daniel." Matthew reeled around to see his wife standing to the far side of the platform, calling her son.

As he stood, he called to her, "Jane, Jane it's me." She looked so beautiful and young, but like Daniel, she didn't even notice him.

Without batting an eye, she gently continued, "Daniel, come on honey. They want to close up, and besides, your father will wonder what took us so long."

"Mom!" Daniel said as he got up and ran to her. "I prayed real good this time, and I told God that you were praying too and that two prayers counted for a whole lot. Mom, do you think it counts as many as a bazillion?"

"Maybe, Daniel, maybe," his mother quietly replied, and she put her arm around him as they walked down the small aisle and out the side door of the church.

Matthew walked back to the front of the platform, sat down on the front edge of the stage, and stared at the altar where his son had just pleaded for his soul. He didn't even notice that the carpenter had sat down beside him.

"Amazing that a little child could know and understand so much while his father doesn't even have a clue."

Matthew glanced up, wiping his face. "Thank God for moms."

At that the carpenter gave a great big grin.

"What," asked Matthew? "What's so funny?"

"Bazillions?"

"Yeah, I guess he got something from me."

"Oh, you'll find he got more from you than you think."

"Sure he did."

The carpenter just stood there looking at him, shaking his head and still wearing that wonderful grin. As Matthew sat there on the edge of the platform, the scene started to change. There were people in a few of the pews and several kneeling on the bench. Carreen came alongside each one as they prayed.

Matthew was startled when he heard an older man softly praying right next to him. He had seemed to appear out of thin air. His head was bowed, and he was kneeling at the front edge of the platform. As Matthew turned back toward the altar, he was startled to see Daniel again, kneeling and softly praying. He could see his lips moving, but he couldn't make out the sounds.

This was his son Daniel not as he was several years ago but as he was now. A good-looking, strong, self-assured 15-year-old. Matthew couldn't remember when it happened, but it seemed like Daniel changed overnight from a sensitive and shy child, from a child other children enjoyed picking on, to this self-confident, bright, caring young man. Sure, playing football had strengthened his body, but Daniel now possessed something much more than outward strength. He was in youth leadership at church and a madrigal choir in school, and he even got a lead role in the school musical.

As he stared at his son he now knew what had transformed him. It was his faith and relationship with God. Matthew remembered telling Daniel that he was the most religious kid he knew. Daniel would always reply, "It's not religion, Dad. It's my relationship with God that matters."

Matthew had always thought of religion or "a relationship with God" as a crutch, but Daniel saw God as his own personal trainer — pushing him, stretching him, preparing him for the trials he would have to face. And face them he did, many times alone.

Matthew looked into his son's face and saw such love and compassion that he could only sit there and marvel. Daniel's eyes suddenly opened, startling Matthew as he stood up. Daniel looked right at his father, but Matthew felt his son staring right through him.

"Father," Daniel began, with a strong, rich voice. "Thank you for loving me, caring for me, and helping me grow. You and you alone have always been there to comfort and guide me."

Matthew was very perplexed. He saw the carpenter heading toward him. Matthew said to him, "I did love and care for my son, but I wasn't always there. I don't understand."

The carpenter pointed behind Matthew. He turned and saw a large cross hanging from the wall at the back of the platform. As Daniel continued, Matthew stepped to the side to watch and listen to his son pray to his heavenly father. He noticed Carreen was already standing behind Daniel with her hand on the back of his head.

"You know all things, and with you all things are possible," Daniel continued as tears began to form in the corners of his eyes. "I have seen you work in many of my friends' lives and even some teachers at school, but every time I think my dad is opening up to you something happens and he becomes distant again. Then I push too hard and he walks away. God, I want my dad to know you so badly. Sometimes I feel I'm getting in the way. We don't connect like we used to. Something I can't fight is pulling him further and further away. It's just been so long . . . sometimes I'm afraid it won't happen at all. Help me be a better son so he will see you living in me. Help me to show your joy and love. Even if you have to use someone else to reach him, I don't care how you do it just save him." Then Daniel sunk to his knees and started to cry.

Matthew knelt down in front of him and put his hand on his shoulder, and even though he knew Daniel couldn't hear him, he spoke to his son. "Daniel, God answered your prayers. I accepted Jesus in my life. I just wish I hadn't waited till the last minute. You were never the problem—it was me."

Matthew looked down for a moment, gathering his thoughts, and then he looked straight into Daniel's eyes through the moisture in his own. "Thank you, big guy, for pushing when you did or I might not be here now. Son, thank you for never giving up on me."

At that Daniel looked up with tears still running down his face. Tears that Matthew would have hidden and been ashamed of, but not Daniel; he didn't care what other people thought. He was going after God. Daniel was looking at the cross again. "God, will it ever happen?"

As those last words left Daniel's lips the scene started to fade. Matthew found himself kneeling by the railing on the porch of his home.

"Don't you think God would do everything possible to answer Daniel's prayers?" came the carpenter's voice from behind him.

Matthew turned and nodded.

The carpenter seemed to be looking off in the distance. "Isn't it beautiful?"

Puzzled, Matthew looked out at the countryside. "Yeah, it's all beautiful."

The carpenter continued, "The hand of God at work, that's the real beauty. How he changes a willing life and then uses that life to change yet another life. Matthew, can you count the seeds in an apple?"

"Sure, as long as you don't swallow them," replied Matthew.

"How about the number of apples in a seed?" asked the ever-smiling carpenter.

"Nobody can know that."

"God can!"

Matthew started to understand. "I guess my son is bearing a lot of fruit," he said with a big grin of his own. "He's such a great kid, always thinking about others —visiting his sick friend with soup, helping to clean the church... I remember when he would ask if there was anything he could do to help me! Is that what God does in your life? I mean, like helping you to not always think of yourself, but to think of others. I wish I could tell him thanks and let him know how I feel."

All of a sudden Matthew's countenance changed as he realized, "Daniel doesn't know. My son doesn't know that I'm here! All he knows is that I was murdered. Because I waited till the last minute... he may think I'm in hell."

Hell. The word alone made Matthew shudder. He looked into the carpenter's eyes. "What will happen to Daniel if he thinks his prayers weren't answered? He'll blame God. I know I would. Couldn't there have been...." His voice cracked as he fell to his knees and started to sob. "What have I done?"

The carpenter knelt beside Matthew. "There was no other way. Your wife and son are strong now. It was time," he said with those caring eyes, piercing Matthew's soul.

"Won't Daniel blame God? What if he starts to think there is no God?" Matthew said, feeling his heart welling up in his throat.

"He might for a while." The carpenter got up and walked across the porch to the steps. He motioned for Matthew to follow, and they both walked down the steps onto the path across the meadow. "Matthew, Daniel is strong."

"But, how do you know that he is strong, strong enough to overcome the stumbling block I put in his way?" Matthew asked with a tremble still in his voice.

"Because I asked the Father to make him strong."

Chapter 19 –Prayer Warrior

Daniel could feel his mother's tension. She didn't even notice when he walked over to the kitchen to get the cell off the charger. He silently prayed as he started speed dialing people from church. *Dear God please let Charlie be home.*

The Thompsons lived only two blocks away at the entrance to their development. *Come on Charlie; be home, not at the club house.*

Two rings. "Please God, please... Charlie! I don't have much time. I need you to drive me and Mom to Memorial. Dad's been in an accident... Great... I don't know... I don't know... No, I'm calling him next ... Just drive our car. We don't have time. Be there in a minute. Mom's heading for the car, thanks."

Daniel clicked off the cell, and his hand started to shake. He grabbed his backpack and chased after his mom, who had just grabbed her purse and shot out the door. He ran around to the passenger's side, threw his backpack in, and jumped in the front seat.

His mom's red swollen eyes met his. "Pray, Daniel, pray."

"I am, Mom. Stop at Charlie's on the way out—he said he would drive."

Jane looked at Daniel but quickly crumbled under the load she felt. "You're right," she said as she quickly glanced both ways and blasted through the intersection.

They both saw the sixty-three year old Charlie walking down the middle of the street toward them, dressed in mechanic's overalls.

Jane pulled to the curb, put the Honda Pilot in park, and got out. "You're the best, Charlie," Jane said, giving him a small hug.

"I called the prayer chain," Charlie said as he opened the back door for Jane. "I hope that was okay."

Daniel opened the passenger's door and got in the back to be with his mom. "Overalls?" he asked Charlie.

Charlie buckled himself in. "I have a new project, a 59 El Camino. Don't you worry, Miss Jane, your Matthew will be fine," Charlie said as he sped out of the development.

Daniel noticed his mom's hands were shaking.

Jane just stared into space as thoughts of Matthew dying raced through her mind. "Daniel, I don't even know… I'm afraid we'll get there and the doctor will hold my hand and say how sorry he is. That they tried everything, but…"

Jane looked over and saw Daniel praying. "My little prayer warrior," she said and ran her hand through his thick hair. "God help us."

She got on her cell and called her mom, pastor, and a few others, giving them all the same brief message: "Matthew's hurt, we're on our way to Memorial. Pray and ask others to pray. Got to go."

In no time, Charlie was pulling up at the emergency entrance to Memorial. Jane and Daniel were met by several members of their church.

"I got a call from Pastor and came right away," said Susan. "Pastor's on his way. Others are already here." Susan and Jane sang in the church choir together. She was an awesome intercessor and a dear friend—definitely a wonderful person to have at your side, especially at a time like this.

Daniel grabbed their things and followed his mom and Susan inside.

"They said to come down this side hall," Susan continued. "They have a room set up just for you. They said the doctor…"

Chapter 20 – Matthew 6

As Matthew walked with the carpenter, he thought about all the struggles and difficulties his son had gone through and how God made him stronger through each one. He had to work hard in school; good grades didn't come easy to him. He didn't have many childhood friends and had been mistreated when he was younger. "So... God allowed or even sent Daniel through many of the trials in his life to prepare him for the time when God would answer his prayer for me."

"Something like that, but that's not the only reason." explained the carpenter as they continued down the path. "Daniel desires to touch lives. He needs God's strength to do so, especially when people hurt him. He also longs to follow God's will for his life. God has helped Daniel be battle-ready." Then he stopped and turned toward Matthew. "Strength isn't always enough, particularly when you choose not to use it. That is why discouragement is one of the accuser's most lethal weapons."

"What can I do? Daniel did so much for me. I want to... need to... do something to help him. I have found out that the Word of God and prayer are so powerful. Once you get to Heaven are you still allowed to pray? Can I pray for my son?"

The carpenter just shook his head and gave him a what-am-I-going-to-do-with-you smile.

"Well I'm new to this. I don't even know how to pray... you know, a real prayer." Matthew humbly looked down.

"Well the disciples had some difficulty with prayer. You may want to read about it," said the carpenter as they approached a park bench next to the path.

As Matthew went to sit down, he said, "I don't have a ... what's this?" He almost sat on a package. It looked familiar, but for some reason he couldn't remember. It was a strange feeling not to remember.

"Don't you like surprises?" asked the carpenter as he noticed the look on Matthew's face. "Don't worry; your memory will come back. Open it."

Matthew just stared at the package and noticed a small card made out of the same material as the package. He lifted the flap and read, "Happy Father's Day! Love, your son Daniel." All of a sudden he remembered receiving this gift from Daniel last year, but it was like he was receiving it all over again because, for the life of him, he didn't know what it was. He just sat there looking at it.

"Well, are you going to open it?" asked the carpenter, breaking the silence.

Matthew was always one to rip into packages, but this time he slowly slid his index finger under the seam to undo the tape. As the paper unfolded in front of him, he read, "Holy Bible." It was the New International Version. He removed the rest of the paper, then opened it up and read:

Presented To:	*Dr. Matthew Peterson*
By:	*His Son Daniel*
On:	*Fathers Day*

As he closed the Bible and held it to his chest, he heard Daniel's voice. He didn't know if it was the memory flooding back or what, but he was grateful. "Do you like it, Dad?" came Daniel's words. "It's one of the newer versions, so it's easier to read." Matthew sat there for a moment, letting the words bathe him.

Then he slowly stood up and with a strong, bold voice, as if he wanted all of heaven to hear, he said, "Yes Daniel, I love this Bible! Through it you have given me light and life, hope and love, peace and strength, and more than anything else, a relationship with your God." Then he raised the Bible high with both hands. "These words will help me to know him like you know him so he can work through my life like he has worked through yours." He lowered the Bible, holding it close to his chest. "Thank you, son. May God bless you for it. Thank you God for allowing me to receive something now that I rejected then. Something worth so much that I thought was worth so little. Thank you for restoring this valuable gift to me. I will treasure it always."

After a moment the carpenter said, "I thought you didn't know how to pray?"

"Well that wasn't really praying… was it?" said Matthew. "I thought praying was saying a lot of thee's and thou's and a lot of other things I don't understand."

"If thee's and thou's are a part of your normal speech, then that's okay, but a lot of those prayers are for men, not God," replied the carpenter. "Prayer is just as simple as talking to God. By the way, he loves to hear your voice. How did it make you feel a moment ago when you heard Daniel's voice? God longs to hear your voice even more than that."

"It sounds so easy, and I know God wants me to," replied Matthew. "But I'm not sure where to start. You said that even the disciples had some difficulty with prayer, and there was something I can read that would help."

"It's as easy as talking to your father," said the carpenter with a gleam in his eye.

"But…."

The carpenter interrupted Matthew, "I know it's not easy for everyone because not everyone has had a loving father. Now you know you have a loving father, and now is always a good time to start. We can start in Matthew."

Matthew looked puzzled. He backed up a little bit and looked at himself. "I guess it's okay." He braced himself and closed his eyes.

"You must open your eyes," said the carpenter, trying to contain himself. "I love little children."

"You love little children? What does that have to do with it?" Matthew opened his eyes, still feeling anxious.

"Nothing." said the carpenter. "Ready to get started?"

"Okay," replied Matthew.

"Matthew six," said the carpenter, watching closely to see what Matthew would do.

"Matthew Six," repeated Matthew. "Am I no longer Matthew Peterson?"

"No, No," said the carpenter. "You are still Matthew Peterson, but you want to learn about prayer, so we need Matthew six."

"Matthew Six—isn't that a strange name?" replied Matthew, very seriously.

The carpenter couldn't help himself, and he almost exploded when he said. "What, Matthew?"

Now Matthew knew there was something going on. He felt a laughter welling up inside even though he didn't know why, so he replied. "No Six?"

The carpenter exploded in laughter as he repeated, "No Six." And with tears rolling down his face he asked Matthew to open up his Bible to the beginning.

Matthew promptly opened his Bible and started to read. "I remember this part. 'In the beginning God created the heavens and the earth.'"

The carpenter motioned for him to stop. "That's Genesis. I want you to turn to the beginning of the Bible."

"I thought Genesis *was* the beginning of the Bible," said Matthew.

"Well, how about turning to before the beginning. Go ahead, it's okay," urged the carpenter.

As Matthew started to turn the pages back he said, "I always thought that Genesis was the beginning. It says 'Introduction to Genesis.'" He flipped a few more pages. "The Old Testament."

"Keep going," encouraged the carpenter. "Genesis is the beginning, but before that the publishers may add helps to assist you to read and locate information in it. Many times they add maps and concordances in the back of the Bible."

"Ok, here is the Preface," Matthew said as he continued his backward search. "Then there is one of those help sections on how to use the Bible. Then they have a page of abbreviations. Hey! There's my name and its abbreviation is Mt."

"Keep going," replied the carpenter as he shook his head.

"Then they have pages that help you find maps and articles. Some of these look really fascinating." He stopped to read one of the pages.

"Matthew," said the carpenter.

Matthew looked up. "Oh, yeah. Then there's the table of contents and the dedication."

"Stop… in the table of contents, do you see Matthew?" asked the carpenter.

"Yes, I see it and it has a page number next to it. Wow, I'm in the Bible!" He flipped to the page number. "Okay, I'm at Matthew, now what?"

"Matthew six," replied the carpenter shaking his head. "Chapter six, verses five through fifteen."

"Oh, *that* Matthew six," Matthew said, his head buried in the book. "Okay, starting in verse five. It's in red."

"Some Bibles print the words of Jesus in red," answered the carpenter.

"So these are the words of Jesus," Matthew replied reverently as he eagerly continued. "'And when you pray, do not be like the hypocrites, for they love to pray standing in the synagogues and on the street corners to be seen by men. I tell you the truth; they have received their reward in full. But when you pray, go into your room, close the door and pray to your Father, who is unseen.' So that's why Jane would go to bed earlier; to have some quiet time without me to pray. 'Then your Father, who sees what is done in secret, will reward you. And when you pray, do not keep on babbling like pagans, for they think they will be heard because of their many words. Do not be like them, for your Father knows what you need before you ask him.' If he knows what I need before I ask, why do I need to ask? 'This, then, is how you should pray: Our Father in heaven, hallowed be your name, your kingdom come, your will be done on earth as it is in heaven. Give us today our daily bread. Forgive us our debts, as we also have forgiven our debtors. And lead us not into temptation, but deliver us from the evil one.' He certainly delivered me from the evil one at the gate! 'For if you forgive men when they sin against you, your heavenly Father will also forgive you. But if you do not forgive men their sins, your Father will not forgive your sins.' Wow, that's pretty strong. If we aren't forgiving, he won't forgive us.

"So should I just pray this Prayer?"

"If you agree with and desire everything in that prayer, then it's okay to pray that prayer," replied the carpenter with a look of concern that Matthew hadn't seen before. "But to only recite the prayers of others, even if they are great prayers, doesn't help your relationship with God grow. You would be missing out on your most precious relationship with your Heavenly Father. You can talk to him just like you talk to me."

"You're easy to talk to. You're sincere and honest and you put me at ease. Could you help me start?" asked Matthew as he knelt next to the bench.

"I would be glad to," replied the carpenter as he stood behind Matthew. "Father, this is Matthew, he wants to talk to you and get to know you."

When Matthew heard the carpenter standing behind him he felt a peace baptize him from his head to his toes. "Father, I wish I knew what to say, but there is so much inside of me. I'm glad I don't have to pray on the street corner in front of everyone. Not that I don't want people to know what you have done for me. I really do, but I'm just new at praying and I wouldn't want to make a mistake. I know you are good. Most people don't know it; I didn't, but you really are.

"Take me, for example. Here's this guy that lives his whole life for himself thinking all the time that either you don't exist or that you don't care, or that you only want perfect people. You give this man a loving wife and son who both know you and pray for him all the time, but does he accept you? No, he doesn't. You know that the only way to save this man is to leave him no way out, to strip everything away from him, including his life."

Matthew paused for a moment at the impact of his own words. "Staring death in the face with all hope gone, he calls to you… for you, God of the universe, to save him, and you do. Just like that. You do this knowing that this man's son, who loves you, may blame you, God, for not saving his dad and allowing him to be murdered. You take the blame because of this man…" Matthew's voice cracked. "Me… because of me. All because I didn't accept you sooner. You are so great and good that you sent Raah to help me. In fact, if you hadn't sent him to slice away the fear and doubt I would not have made it here. You gave me a song. You have this carpenter build this home for me, and though I know he must be very busy he has not left my side. He shows me things and explains so much, all with joy and a smile."

Matthew glanced at the carpenter. "Thank you for letting him be the one to show me around. I know he says he's just a carpenter, but to me he's so much more. He's the closest friend and best guide. He's helped me so much. He makes me feel important even though I know, and I think he knows, I've done nothing. He makes me feel wanted. I think he's a lot like you."

"Oh, thanks again for the Bible," Matthew said, holding it close. "I want to read it to get to know you more. I liked what you had to say about prayer. I know you have already done so much for me, but I must ask you to help my son and my wife. I know that they are strong, but they might not understand. Help them; comfort them; send people their way to help them. I don't know if it is okay, but if it's okay for me to ask you to have other people pray for my family I'd... I'd... really appreciate it. I've messed up so much. 'I'm sorry' doesn't explain what I want to say—it seems so small, but you know my heart, how it has changed because of you. My heart aches for others instead of myself. This new ache feels both good and bad.

"God, I hurt for them. Only you can fix what I have broken." As he knelt there quietly, tears streaming down his face, he felt a peace surround him, a peace that somehow assured him everything would be okay. After a while, he looked to the side and saw that the carpenter had sat down next to him and was looking down on him, wearing his wonderful grin.

Chapter 21 - No Accident

As Jane, Daniel, and Susan hurried down the hall they were greeted by a woman wearing a colorful jumpsuit and a warm smile.

"Mrs. Peterson, my name is Naomi; I will be with you throughout tonight. First and most important, your husband is alive and in surgery. I wish I could tell you more."

Jane gave Naomi a hug and started to cry. "That's more than I had a moment ago." Daniel and Susan continued on without her to the waiting room.

"As your friend was saying, as soon as Dr. Gray is out of surgery he will give you a full report. It looks like you have a lot of support; that's very important. Remember, I'm here for you and your son if you need me"

Her gentleness and soft tones comforted Jane. Jane said, "Do you know what happened?"

"Someone from the police department will be talking with you shortly."

Jane froze, *Matthew what did you do.* "I thought it was an accident".

Naomi put her hand on Jane shoulder. "I didn't hear anything about an accident. I'm sure the officer will be able answer your questions."

Daniel came back down the hall. "Mom, come with me. You won't believe this—they have set up a special waiting room just for us!"

Jane entered the special trauma waiting room with Daniel and was immediately surrounded by a dozen praying saints from her church, softly reaching out to God on her and Matthew's behalf.

After a few minutes, Naomi came in and gave Jane a gentle tap on the shoulder to get her attention and whispered, "Need you to come with me. Daniel, I need to borrow your mom for a few minutes. Can you take care of the others while we're gone?"

"Sure."

"Thanks, big guy. We won't be long."

Jane followed Naomi out of the waiting room. "Thanks, its better… that he not…"

"He's a fine young man. He needs time with friends."

"Yes, you're right. Thank you."

They headed down the hall with a blue stripe on the floor and turned right to follow a green stripe.

"Jane, they said an officer was waiting outside waiting room one."

"Will this take long?"

"I don't think so, but if there is any news on your husband, I'll let you know right away."

They headed past the main desk toward the waiting officer.

The officer approached Jane. "Mrs. Peterson?"

"Yes, I'm Mrs. Peterson."

"My name is Officer Wellington. The front desk said we could use the doctor's lounge."

Naomi stepped up and said, "Good afternoon, officer. My name is Naomi. If you will follow me, the doctor's lounge is just around the corner." Naomi led Jane and Officer Wellington to the lounge. "This will give you both a little privacy. There is water and soda in the fridge. Help yourself. Officer, please let me know when you're through."

"Thank you, Naomi."

"You're welcome." And with a click of the door, Jane and Officer Wellington were alone.

The officer placed his briefcase on one chair. "Would you like something to drink?"

Jane sat down, "No, thank you."

"Very well," Officer Wellington said as he pulled his clipboard from his briefcase. "Ma'am, I'm very sorry to have to bother you right now with these details, but we have to get your statement as soon as possible. It may help in apprehending the perpetrators."

"Perpetrators?"

"Ma'am, has anyone told you anything?"

"All I know is that Matthew was in an accident and was flown in by helicopter."

"I see...does your husband have..."

"Have what? He's in perfect health."

"No Ma'am, I didn't mean..."

"It wasn't his fault, was it? Oh my God. Was someone else hurt?"

"No. No one else was hurt. Mrs. Peterson, it wasn't an accident."

Chapter 22 - Scars

"I thought you didn't know how to pray," said the carpenter as Matthew got up off his knees and sat next to him on the bench. "You find out a lot about yourself just talking to him."

"Yeah, it's like he's pulling you out of yourself." said Matthew. "I just never knew how good he is, and it's still hard to comprehend."

"Oh, you will never stop learning about the goodness of the Father," replied the carpenter. "He's very creative."

"Speaking of creative, I need to check out that home you made me," said Matthew with a suspicious eye as he got up and started walking back to his home.

"Matthew, what do you mean?" The carpenter started to follow him. "And after all of those good things you said about me."

"You're good all right, maybe too good... Mr. 'Matthew Six.' You really enjoyed that, didn't you?" Matthew said as he quickened the pace.

"I did enjoy the moment; it was quite pleasurable. Don't worry, your home is perfect," said the carpenter as he started to pass Matthew.

"No surprises?' inquired Matthew as he broke into a run.

"The only way it could be perfect is for it to have surprises," replied the carpenter as he ran after Matthew. "After all, they are so much fun."

Laughing, they tore off down the path through the meadows back to the house. As they approached, Matthew heard the wind rushing through the treetops and started to slow down. "I always loved hearing the wind whistle though the treetops at my grandparents' place. Then it would come down and blow against your face. Sometimes when it was strong I would close my eyes and feel like I was flying."

"The wind here is a little different," remarked the carpenter.

Matthew could hear the wind approach. "How can the wind be dif…" Before he could finish, the wind hit him. Instead of feeling the gentle coolness on his face, he felt it go right through him. It was exhilarating, and it penetrated him so that he couldn't move and could barely breathe except for the occasional gulp.

He felt the wind going through every fiber of his being. He closed his eyes, feeling the wonder. Then almost as soon as it started, it stopped and Matthew almost fell forward.

"Wow. It was different, all right, like… like… Wow!" Matthew exclaimed, his eyes wide open in amazement.

"Part of the wind's job is to be unexplainable, to come and go when and where it will. Just like a bunch of big and small surprises," said the carpenter.

"You really must love your job," declared Matthew, shaking his head.

"It's not a job, Matthew, it's an adventure!" He pat Matthew on the back.

Matthew looked over at the carpenter and saw a terrible scar on the inside of his left wrist, and he instinctively pulled back. "Bad accident?" he asked.

"No, no accident," he said as he showed Matthew both wrists.

"Why are they still there? That couldn't have happened here."

"No, it didn't happen here. I chose to keep them, as a reminder. Hey, aren't you ever going to go inside your house?"

"Sure, I guess I'd better check it out." Matthew was glad to move on to another subject. He bolted up the stairs and across the porch to the front door, and as he was about to turn the knob, he stopped. "After you," he said, motioning the carpenter to go first.

"What, do you think I have the front door booby-trapped? I'm much more creative than that. After all, I'm an artist."

So Matthew decided it was okay, opened the door, and went inside. He stopped for a second when he heard a click and looked up just in time to be doused by a small cup of water. "I thought you said it was okay?" he said and turned back toward the carpenter.

"Right as rain, Matthew. Besides, you enjoy this sort of thing, and you look so refreshed!" said the carpenter through his laughter. "An oldie but a goodie. I heard you were quite the trickster in your day."

"Well maybe just a little bit, but I'm reformed," laughed Matthew as he pushed his wet hair back and started to look around. Everything was beautiful, just as he knew it would be.

The front door opened up into a big great room, which had a table and chairs on one end and a sofa and a chair and ottoman on the other end facing a fireplace. The woodwork on all the walls was a gorgeous natural light oak.

He wanted to explore more of the home, but even more he wanted to explore the Bible, especially the book of Matthew. He placed the Bible down on the table and sat down, almost forgetting the carpenter. "This place is wonderful."

With Matthew watching on, the carpenter raised both arms and said a blessing over Matthew's home. "Dear Father, I thank you for bringing Matthew here and allowing me to build this home for him. I ask you now to breathe your life into this place so that everyone who enters will feel the love, peace, and joy that comes only from you."

As Matthew watched, the carpenter turned to go, as if he knew Matthew needed some time alone, time spent reading and getting to know God. He opened the door. "Enjoy," he said as he flashed Matthew a welcome-home smile.

Matthew returned with a thank-you-for-everything-and-especially-for-being-my-friend smile because words wouldn't come.

"You're very welcome, Matthew," he said as he went out the door. It closed behind him.

Matthew opened the Bible back to Matthew and started to read. He read about the genealogy of Jesus and about Mary and Joseph. He read about the humble and wonderful birth of Jesus and the Magi who visited him, gave him gifts, and worshiped him.

He read how King Herod had the entire baby boy population younger than two years old killed, trying to destroy Jesus, and how an angel appeared to Joseph to warn them to escape to Egypt.

The words seemed to leap off the pages as he read the Sermon on the Mount. Through each page he felt the warmth and love of God being displayed through his son, Jesus. Even though the miracles were great, it was the compassion and love that drew Matthew to each page and beckoned him on to the next.

"How could I have been so dull?" Matthew shook his head as he looked at the words. Words that once seemed weak and worthless were now revealed to show both strength and compassion.

He now understood how blessed the meek, humble, and persecuted were. Matthew also started to understand how strong they were, just like his son, Daniel. He picked up the opened book, placed it on his chest, and felt a warm closeness to his son.

"God, is Daniel strong enough? Is he strong enough not to know I'm here and still trust in you? I was never that strong. My deception led me to place myself at the center, and if bad things happened I would blame them on a God that I didn't believe even existed. I stupidly played it both ways and it almost cost me my soul. Spending time in this book of yours is helping me to understand just how foolish my wisdom was and how great you are. I know you love Daniel more than I could ever know, but…"

Matthew started to cry. It was like the frustrated cry of a child who spelled his own name wrong. Then the realization hit him that he and God had a special relationship. He and God were both Daniel's fathers.

Through his tears, Matthew cried out, "As Daniel's heavenly Father you knew who I was and you still let me be his earthly father. I haven't done a very good job, but you know how much I love him, care for him, and long to see him again. God, don't let mistakes I made harm him. Draw him into Your Word. Bring other believers to his side to help him. Draw Daniel close to his mother. Give Jane wisdom and understanding. Most of all give them hope, hope that I am with you… I miss them… I want them to… to… know… to know I'm okay. I know your Spirit speaks to their hearts. Spirit let them know… please let them know."

Things seemed to slow like a silent pause, waiting for Matthew to continue. "God, I don't know what should be in a prayer and what shouldn't, but I just want to say… I'm just trying to say… I … I love you. I know you know that I do. I just wanted you to hear it. Thank you for hearing my prayer… This is Matthew."

Chapter 23 – What If

"What do you mean it wasn't an accident?"

With a momentary silence Officer Wellington walked over to the fridge. "You sure I can't get you something?"

Jane's mouth was dry with the shock. "Yes, water would be fine. I'm sorry; it's hard to even think."

He handed her the cold bottle. "It's a hard thing to go through, ma'am. You're doing better than most."

"What do you mean it wasn't an accident?" she repeated.

"Does your husband carry his wallet in his back pocket?"

"I was told it was an accident."

"No, ma'am, this was no accident. His wallet, did he carry it in his back pocket?"

"Yes, I think so. What does where he carries his wallet have to do with anything?"

"We believe he was robbed, unless someone wanted it to look that way. Does your husband have any enemies?"

Jane's voice slowed as she pushed out the words. "Robbed? Enemies? No, he's a great guy."

"His wallet is missing and his back pocket was torn."

"What happened? I thought he was in a car accident."

Officer Wellington flipped back to the front of his notepad. "I don't believe a car was involved. A fire alarm was set off at the Northfield Clinic and a fire truck was dispatched from Highland Station to respond. They arrived, sighting no smoke or odor. Office worker alerted fire chief of someone hurt in the parking garage. Fire chief found your husband and called for paramedics and backup. We responded and secured the site as paramedics prepared for transport.

Heliport rescue one was in the vicinity and was on the ground in minutes. I was assigned to Mr. Peterson, so once I turned over the scene to the crime unit I came here. My first concern is his continued safety and then to gather what information I can."

"His... safety?"

"It's just a normal precaution. He's been through enough. You all have. That's why I have to ask the things I ask."

"About enemies?"

"Yes, it's something I have to ask."

"I understand."

Office Wellington got up and opened the door. "Thanks, ma'am. Not everyone does."

Jane wiped the tears from her eyes as she left the room. "Was he conscious when you saw him?"

"I wasn't that close ma'am, but I don't think so. I can tell you one thing—that fire alarm saved your husband's life."

Jane tried to compose herself. "Please let me know when you find out what happened."

"Yes, ma'am," said Officer Wellington as he turned, heading down the hall toward the nurses' station.

"Jane!" Doctor Aims, Matthew's colleague from the clinic, burst through the emergency doors with Anne following close behind. "Anne and I took a taxi as soon as they finished taking our statements. Any word on Matthew?"

"He's still in surgery."

Anne ran past the doctor into Jane's arms.

"I'm so sorry," she said, bursting into tears.

Doctor Aims continued down the hall. "I'll get an update on Matthew's status and check on Martha."

"Martha?"

Anne pushed her tears away as Jane continued towards the waiting room. "Poor Martha, she's still pretty upset. She found Matthew and is having a pretty hard time of it. They brought her in for observation."

"Anne, what happened?"

"Best we can tell is Matthew was attacked in the parking garage right after he left the office."

"I'm confused. I thought the fire chief found Matthew."

"That was after... when..."

Jane just realized that she was pushing too hard and too fast. "Let's sit for a bit."

"Thanks," Anne said as they crossed the hallway and sat down on the empty bench across from the snack machines.

"Can I get you a drink, Anne?"

Anne usually always refused, but her throat was very dry. "Water, please."

Jane had already grabbed a crisp new one dollar bill from her wallet. She touched Anne's shoulder as she got up. "Thanks."

"Thanks?"

Jane slipped the bill into the machine and punched H5 and grabbed the bottle of water. "I feel so helpless. It just feels good to be useful."

Anne heaved a sigh. "Thanks."

Jane sat down with her arm around Anne as she took a drink. "Lord, thank you for my sister and for using her to bring help for Matthew. Give her peace and strength. Amen."

Anne gave Jane a hug and took another drink. "We had a fire alarm about ten minutes after he left. Martha, poor thing, wanted to take off a little early. She found him lying between two cars on her way out. I thought the fire alarm was one of his little pranks, scheduling a surprise fire alarm for right... I'm sorry, Jane."

"The officer said it may have saved his life."

"I don't think he did it. The fire chief swears it wasn't on the schedule."

"On the schedule or not, thank God it happened."

"I'm better now," Anne said as they both started to stand.

"Daniel and the others are in a room they set up for us down the hall."

"Others?" Anne asked as they headed down the hall.

"Daniel made a few calls and they came for support. It's amazing. They already had a room set up for us. Good thing because it's pretty full."

Daniel joined his mother as she and Anne entered the room.

"What if there wasn't a fire alarm, Anne? What if Martha didn't leave early or didn't see him?"

Daniel wrapped his arm around his mom. "But those things did happen, Mom, and he's still with us."

Chapter 24 – Parable of the Mask

Matthew just sat there in his silence not even wiping the tears from his face. He didn't even notice that the carpenter had entered the room.

"Here, let me get that." The carpenter was at his side, wiping his tears with a soft cloth. "I don't think you need any help learning how to pray".

"How long have you been here?"

"You know me; I'm here and there and everywhere. I did get to hear the good part. I really liked how you ended your prayer. Someone said once that you must become as a little child."

"That sounds like something Jesus would say."

"Sounds like you've been reading."

Matthew was still holding the open Bible to his chest. He held it out to the carpenter. "The more I read, the more I want to know. Why did the religious leaders hate Jesus when all he did was love and heal the hurting? They would try to trick him, but every time it backfired and the people followed Jesus even more. Jesus loved. He just loved! He loved the blind, the sick, the lame, the rich, the poor, the tax collectors, even the leper. Sure many of them needed healing but their bodies were only a small part of the healing that took place. For maybe the first time in their lives someone had cared just for them."

"Matthew, would you like hear a story?" the carpenter asked as he sat down next to him, "It's about Jesus."

"Sure." Matthew's eyes sparkled with anticipation. "I hope you're a good storyteller."

"Well… I never!" The carpenter flashed Matthew one of his I-can't-believe-you-said-that smiles. And for emphasis, he shook his head.

"You never... you never what? You've never told a story...
Then I'm your guinea pig!" Matthew snorted with laughter at his own
cleverness.

"Are you a happy guinea pig?" the carpenter said as he too
started to laugh.

Matthew shook his head. "I'll just listen now."

The carpenter stood facing Matthew as he started the story.

* * *

*"Unclean, unclean!" The words that came from the leper's
mouth would ring in his ears to remind not only others but also him of
who he was. As the disease ate away at his body, the words ate away
at his soul.*

*Once the leprosy spread to his face, his friends and family
wouldn't even look at him. The only touch he would ever receive was
the touch of his own numb, swollen hands.*

*When he was hungry he would yell out to a crowd, "Unclean,
food for the unclean."*

*Among the jeers and curses someone would throw him some
bread. Many times the bread would be ground into the dust, or mud,
because food for the "unclean" should be "unclean."*

*No one knew or cared who he was anymore; he was alone. He
tried to pray to God but was told, time after time, that this curse was
from God. Surely God wouldn't listen to someone he had cursed?*

*Even so, this leper would still talk to God; he had no one else.
Day after day he would cry out to God in sorrow for anything and
everything he had done in his life. He had been a proud man, but no
more. Now humility and sorrow were his only companions.*

Matthew could picture the lepers with their sores, wrapped and
calling out *unclean, unclean* as the law required. The carpenter's eyes
were solemn, but then his face started to change and a smile started to
emerge as he continued.

*Today the crowd was much larger than usual and everyone was
talking. Some were talking about a teacher. Others were talking
about a healer. Still other voices, angry voices, spoke of blasphemy*

and the law; so many voices and everyone trying to push their way to the middle of the mass of people.

The leper strained to hear the words coming from an excited woman. Her voice was so shrill it could be heard above the other sounds, and it was piercing, and to make matters worse the voice was that of a Galilean, slurred and high-pitched.

He strained to hear that one lone voice, which was talking about a healer. She said she saw a blind man, a blind man who was healed!

When he heard it, he felt a strange sensation. The blind are under a curse, are they not? If the blind can be healed, why not the unclean? He felt the strange sensation again. This time he knew what it was. It was hope, hope that just maybe…

The leper had not noticed that he too was being pulled toward the crowd by some invisible source.

"UNCLEAN! You are required to yell UNCLEAN! You filthy dog! You are too close!"

The leper leapt back as if slapped in the face. For a moment he did not know what to do. Instinctively, the words rang from his lips: "Unclean, unclean, bread for the unclean. Unclean, bread for the un—"

The crowd had stopped. His unfinished word caught in his mouth as sound seemed to leave his ears. All he could hear was the beating of his heart. People were turning toward him and pointing. As hearing came back to him, the rest of the word that had been caught in his throat flowed from his lips: "Clean."

The man who had been yelling at him stopped and turned toward the multitude. There was a commotion among the people. A small group in the crowd was heading his way, and as they got closer, the crowd split.

Jesus had indeed heard the man and felt his pain of loneliness and shame. Jesus, ignoring the jeers and hatred surrounding the leper, walked through the people toward his lone cry.

Tears were now streaming down the leper's face, soaking the cloth that hid the horror. "Unclean… unclean," he called out. Jesus reached out his hand toward him. "No, I'm unclean," he cried through the tears and humiliation, trying to get away.

The leper turned and started to run like a trapped animal, but as he did he heard footsteps and the crowd yelling "No!", then gasping as Jesus caught the young man who appeared so old because of his disfigurement. The sea of humanity surrounded the pair. The leper was shaking his head and sobbing, "Unclean, unclean" as Jesus wrapped his arms around him.

Jesus continued comforting the leper—not worried about the mob, not worried about the disease, not worried about the time or about what anyone thought. His concern was for the young man before him. After a while the sobbing of a lifetime of loneliness and disgrace slowly became a whimper.

When Jesus took off the bandages from the young leper's face, the leper instinctively put his hands up to hide his disfigurement and found that his face was smooth to the touch. The leper unwrapped the cloth from his hands to get a better feel and reached again for his face. He could feel the warm tears as his hands caressed his cheeks, and the crowd exploded into joy and laughter. It was like his hands and face were long lost friends getting to know each other all over again. People cheered and started to hug each other.

There was a disturbance in the crowd again. "Let us through! Let us through!" As the sea of people parted, men with long flowing robes emerged, robes which denoted religious leadership.

"What is going on here!" demanded the man who was leading the small group.

This didn't bother Jesus in the least. It was as if he knew they would be there. He just put up his hand and there was silence.

"I tell you the truth. The kingdom of God is like two men, which had leprosy. One day they both found masks, which hid their disease. They were able to walk among the people as they always had but they could never reveal who they really were. They lived with the pain and curse, alone, unable to tell anyone. Fear became their friend, waiting for them at every corner, until one day when their king approached calling them by name. They didn't know how he knew, but somehow he knew all about them. He told them that he also knew about the pain and fear. He said that only they could remove their masks. He promised to heal their disease if they would trust him and take off their masks. One leper started to remove his mask, and as he did the other started to scream and ran away. The king did as he promised. The first leper was not only cleansed but also welcomed into his household."

Jesus rose quietly toward the religious men and held out his hands to them. "Be clean."

"You... you, who just touched a leper, talk to us about being clean!" screamed one of the men, his face turning crimson. "Why do you always talk in riddles? Why can't you talk plainly?"

To this Jesus replied, "He who has an ear let him hear what the spirit is saying to the churches."

* * *

"Well guinea pig, how did I do?" said the carpenter, beaming. It broke Matthew out of the scene.

"Wow, that was… was… well… you know… powerful. Jesus cut right through everything that was happening and went right to the truth. That short story that Jesus told, what was that called?"

"The Parable of the Mask."

"Yeah, that parable was about everyone. I remember the mask I had. The worse I became the better it looked. Sometimes, in fact many times, it had me fooled, but down deep I knew exactly what it hid. I carried so much pain for so long. God is good!"

"All the time," replied the carpenter as he opened the door. "Gotta go."

Matthew raised his hand as his friend disappeared. So many thoughts were racing through his mind, thoughts that were hard to understand.

Jesus loved the people so much, but the religious leaders didn't care for the people, which upset Jesus. Didn't Jesus call those leaders thieves and tip over the tables at the market they had set up within the temple walls? As Matthew read on he found out that they plotted against Jesus and paid one of his disciples to betray him.

Betray Jesus? How…why would anyone betray someone who did so much good? Unfortunately, Matthew knew many men who would have done the same thing. He himself was one of them. How many times did Matthew not like someone or distrust them because they were too good to be true? He always thought they had a hidden agenda because he usually did. If Matthew had been there, he knew he would probably have liked Jesus at first and then rejected him just like the crowds had.

Chapter 25 – Grab and Go

As the hours passed Naomi continued to check on Jane and Daniel. She approached Jane. "He's still fighting," came the comforting words from Naomi followed by a hug and a smile while she surveyed the group.

"Lisa, can you get these nice people more ice?"

Lisa, Naomi's assistant, nodded, grabbed the ice bucket, and left the room.

"Jane, the doctors are cleaning up and will see you and Daniel shortly, if you like."

"Doctors?"

"Yes, they called in a neurosurgeon. It's very common if there is any head trauma, just to be safe. I believe he hit his head pretty hard."

"Head trauma! Oh Matthew what did they do to you? Can I… we see him?"

Just then a doctor entered the room.

"Hi Naomi, this must be Mrs. Peterson." He took Jane's hand in both of his and gave her an assuring smile. "I'm Doctor Allison, head of the trauma team. Your husband is one tough cookie."

"Doctor, how is he? Can we see him?"

"The rest of the team is finishing up; we still need to run a few tests. Most of it's routine. The more we know, the better."

"Doctor, I've set up the next room for you and Doctor Gray. Do you mind, Jane? It will give you and the doctors a little privacy."

Jane nodded with a *this is it* lump in her throat.

Anne walked over and gave Jane's hand a squeeze. "Go ahead, Jane; you and Daniel go do what you need to do. I'll take care of everyone here. Besides, I think I could use a little more prayer time."

Naomi took Jane's arm just like an old friend. "Thanks, Anne. Could you get Daniel for us?" she whispered as she shuffled Jane out the crowded room down the hall with Doctor Allison in tow.

"You are really blessed, Jane, to have such great friends."

That brought a smile to Jane's face. "They are the best, aren't they?"

Naomi and Jane turned back to Doctor Allison as Daniel caught up to the group.

"Daniel, glad you could join us. Doctor Allison, Daniel. Daniel, Doctor Allison."

"Hi. How's my dad?" Daniel asked, a little out of breath.

"He's fighting for all he's worth, son."

"Sounds like dad."

As they continued down the hallway, Naomi glanced back. "You still a Pepper, doc?'

"Of course," Doctor Allison said with a smile.

"Got ya all set up."

"Extra ice?"

"Of course."

"You still doing the Dew, Daniel?"

Daniel shook his head. "You don't miss a thing."

"Just like your mom, Daniel, just like your mom."

Daniel smiled "You might not know that I'm cross-generational and have also gone under a Pepper alias."

Naomi asked Jane, "Translation?"

"He'll have a Dr Pepper."

"See, Naomi," Doctor Allison said as he opened the door. "There's hope for the next generation after all."

The room was arranged with a large oblong table in the middle, with several comfortable chairs. One wall had three sets of light racks for viewing x-rays and MRIs. On the other side was a wet bar with a small refrigerator and microwave behind it.

Daniel entered the room. "Wow!"

"Why don't you peppers have a seat? Jane and I will get the drinks and a few snacks while we wait for Doctor Gray."

"Why wait for that old guy?" came a voice behind them.

Naomi turned toward the door. "Jane and Daniel, meet Doctor Gray."

Doctor Allison nudged Daniel. "Ten bucks says he goes for the Ginger Ale."

"Naomi, I believe I'll be doing the Dew this evening."

"What!" Doctor Allison and Daniel said in unison.

"What can I say? I'm just a cross-generational kind of guy."

Doctor Gray walked over to the table and took a seat. "Any hope for my generation, Danny?"

Daniel looked at both doctors. "Scary."

"I'm a neurosurgeon, Daniel; I'm supposed to know everything. Doctor Allison just makes it easy when he leaves his comm. badge on.

"Great."

"Your team thought it was a hoot."

Doctor Allison removed the small unit from his jacket pocket and switched from send to two-way.

The unit jumped to life, transmitting a quick burst of laughter, followed by silence. "Are we having fun?" Doctor Allison said into the unit.

Silence, followed by, "Working post-op sir," with muffled laughter in the background.

Doctor Allison spoke into the unit, "Good work," then pulled it away. "Doctor Gray, could you pass me some of those Buffalo wings."

"Wings?"

"Gotta go." Doctor Allison smiled as he clicked off the small comm. unit and placed it back in his pocket.

Daniel looked puzzled. "We don't have any wings."

"Oh, my mistake."

Doctor Gray just shook his head.

Jane and Naomi brought in the drinks and a bowl of chips.

Once Jane was seated, Naomi stood next to the wet bar as Doctor Allison started.

"First and most important, we were able to stabilize Matthew."

Tears started forming in Jane's eyes. "Thank you."

"I appreciate that, but I don't want you to think we're out of the woods yet. We were all very fortunate to have one of the best trauma teams in the country on duty today." His eyes lit up as he spoke of his team.

Doctor Allison took a sip of his soda. "He was revived once just before transport. The transport medics lost him a second time and were not able to revive while en route, so the trauma team set up a portable crash unit on the helipad. They jumped in the copter as it touched down; he was still belted in when they revived him. They told me later they modified a procedure they saw performed by a rescue unit they competed against at the Trauma Trials in Florida just three weeks ago. They call it 'grab and go.'"

Daniel asked, "The procedure?"

Doctor Allison laughed. "No, stealing other people's stuff. I wouldn't be surprised if they were on the horn with the rescue squad from Tulsa right now. They sure earned their pay today."

Jane rubbed her hands together. "He's not out of the woods?"

"I'm afraid not. He lost a lot of blood, suffered a broken rib, and punctured a lung. Our main concern with these wounds is infection and trauma to the local organs. Best we can tell is he was stabbed just below the rib cage and was thrown backwards, which caused trauma to the back of the head. Doctor Gray?"

"We already ran a preliminary CATSCAN and MRI. There was the expected local trauma at the back of the head. There were also micro tears to the frontal and left cranial area, which brings us to one of our main concerns: swelling. The brain is completely encased within the skull. There is a normal amount of pressure inside, but a significant amount of added pressure could cause complications. I would like to perform a procedure that will allow us to monitor the pressure and alleviate some of the pressure if swelling should occur."

Jane was now holding Daniel's hand. "Is this procedure dangerous?"

Doctor Gray continued, "Any procedure to the body, let alone the brain, has the potential to be dangerous. Among the many things we can do, this is the least invasive and has very good results. We would drill a small hole in his forehead around his hairline and install a small sensor, called a bolt, to monitor cranial pressure. This small sensor can also be opened to relieve pressure if needed. Right now we're flying blind."

"Can't he just tell us?"

"Right now he's sedated. The main risk, although slight, is infection. On the positive side, I perform this procedure several times a month and many families have found a sense of comfort being able to watch and monitor the pressure."

"Daniel, what do you think?"

"We need to do it, Mom."

"I think you're right."

"Good. Naomi, can you get the needed paperwork?" Doctor Gray said.

Doctor Allison took a sip of his drink and looked at Naomi as she started to leave. "Naomi?"

She paused, her hand on the door. "Yes?"

"Why don't you meet us in recovery six? I think these good people would like to see Matthew."

"Yes!" Daniel jumped out of his chair, ready to go.

Naomi turned to leave. "I'll see you in a few minutes."

Doctor Allison downed the rest of his Dr Pepper. "Thanks, Naomi."

Everyone headed for the door. Naomi took a left toward admin while Doctor Allison and his little band took a right, heading for recovery six.

"Other than a little pale, Matthew looks good, but I must warn you we have him hooked up to every wire and tube you can think of."

Jane grabbed Daniel's arm as they both nodded.

Doctor Allison stopped with his hand on the doorknob. "Even though he's unconscious, it's good to talk to Matthew. Use soft, soothing tones. When he comes to he won't remember what happened or where he is. He needs to know he's safe in the hospital, that he was hurt, and that he's going to be fine."

Chapter 26 -Witness

Matthew was surprised to read that Jesus knew and told his disciples that he would be handed over to be crucified and that he even knew who would betray him. He was even more surprised that he had never heard that before. During the Last Supper, Jesus told all of his disciples that his blood would be poured out for many for the forgiveness of sins.

Later that night, Judas betrayed Jesus with a kiss, and Jesus called him friend. When the soldier came and grabbed Jesus, Peter, one of the disciples, struck one of them with his sword, cutting off his ear. Jesus told Peter to put his sword away because this must happen. Jesus told him if he wanted, he could call on his father to send thousands of angels, but that was not the plan. The plan was for him to die.

Matthew got up and softly laid the Bible down on the small table next to the front door and walked out onto the porch. He sat on the top step, trying to understand. God's plan was for Jesus to die. *Why?* he quietly asked himself as he gazed out over the countryside.

Almost immediately he started to see shadows. Shadows of all kinds of things: people, homes, walls, roads, horses, and trees. As soon as he started to make out the shadows of one scene, another would appear. Soon hundreds and maybe even thousands of shadowy scenes were converging on him. He could see nothing but a murky grayness moving about him.

Matthew sat in silence until he heard the laughter. He placed his hands on the deck to help himself up, only to find that he was now sitting on a rock, one partly made of sandstone that would crumble at the touch.

What was this place? He couldn't imagine there being such a dark place as this in heaven. The laughter was all around him now. First he heard the men, then the women. Their laughter was loud and contagious. There was a sea of people all pushing and shoving.

Matthew could feel their bodies next to his as they bumped and shoved each other, laughing all the while. One would yell, "Save yourself" and push someone else, who would yell back, "He can't" and the laughing would get even louder. Everything seemed so silly, he couldn't help but start to laugh. Sometimes a whole group would ask the question and another group would reply and Matthew would be pushed further into the crowd.

Finally, through the laughter, Matthew asked, "Who is 'he'?" For a brief moment, everyone stopped and looked at Matthew.

Then a huge man said, "Exactly! Who is he?" and shoved Matthew so hard he flew through the crowd to an opening and then onto the ground.

Matthew tried to catch his fall with his hands, but he slipped in the mud and his face and side landed square in the middle of it. Matthew heard someone yell from behind him, "Get back!" Then a large hand grabbed him, lifting him off the ground and throwing him back to the edge of the crowd. "Stay back" was all Matthew heard as he saw the end of a spear thrust in front of his face. All the laughter turned into horror as he looked past the guard and saw his friend, the carpenter, his arms and hands being stretched out on a rough wooden beam.

Matthew stared in horror as he saw the heavy mallet come down on the spike. "NO!" He felt the word in his throat, but all he heard was the sound of the mallet driving the spike through flesh and wood and the screaming of the crowd. He couldn't bear to look. He buried his face in the mud and earth and tried desperately to cover his ears.

Then he felt a hand on his shoulder—a very strong hand but also a very gentle one. He looked up and immediately recognized his guardian Raah. Through the noise and chaos he could hear his friend, even though he never raised his voice.

"You must watch," Raah said, compassion in his voice.

"I can't," Matthew explained as he stared at the foot of the cross.

"He wants you to."

"Why?"

"Because you are his friend and he wants you to be a witness."

At this, Matthew's will crumbled, and his heart broke. He looked up into his Raah's eyes. "Will you help me?"

Without a word, his guardian placed one arm around Matthew's shoulders and the other on his chest, pulling Matthew to his feet. Matthew saw the soldiers drop the heavy beam of the cross into a hole.

"I don't know what to do… I can't help… I can't…" Just then he caught Jesus staring at him with such love. A love that consumed Matthew and pushed everything from his mind so nothing else existed. While this love flowed from Jesus' eyes into Matthew's soul, he found that he couldn't look or think about anything or anyone else.

He could see Jesus' arm spasm as he tried to lift himself for another breath. His eyes closed, and the pain from the spikes sent tremors throughout his body. Then his eyes opened and he looked at Matthew.

"Father, forgive them, for they know not what they do."

The words rang in Matthew's ears. "No, don't!" Matthew said as tears raced down his face and dropped to the mud below. He felt like the leper just before Jesus touched him. He looked into those beautiful, loving eyes. "I don't deserve…"

Father, forgive them, for they know not what they do. Jesus's words echoed in Matthew's mind. Then the voice of the Accuser shot through the jeering crowd.

"Forgiven? Never!"

In the background, he could still hear the jeers and mocking. The carpenter coughed, tried his best to rise, exhaled, and gasped air to speak.

The crowd yelled and cursed. Then the scene changed, and memories and scenes began to cycle rapidly before him. Matthew closed his eyes and was back at a scene where a bully from the 4th grade punched him in the nose because he didn't give him his lunch. The bully and a crowd of 4th graders were laughing as the scene changed to a restaurant he had visited so often. At first, Matthew didn't even notice her sitting in a booth tucked in the back next to a hall leading to the restrooms. Carreen whispered, but he could hear and feel her word's impact.

"Forgiven?"

Matthew knew he needed to forgive the bully. Then without notice the jeers and taunts at Jesus started to drown out everything. He turned toward the sound and saw him. The Accuser was sitting far on the other side, smiling as he held his mouth open, letting the sounds of hatred out.

Matthew yelled with all of his might, "Forgiven!" It caused the Accuser to falter.

The scene changed again. He was watching himself stand next to a register at Tomies, a local fast food restaurant, as Sally Fulton opened the cash drawer next to him and took out a twenty. He was watching the register for Doug, who had to go to the back to get coins. He confronted her about it. The next day he was fired because she said he took the money, and later her boyfriend almost beat her up. He blinked and the Accuser was in front of him. He looked different, but he kept his mouth open with the deafening laugh. Then Matthew heard it again like the clinking of clear crystal when someone chimed for a toast.

"Forgiven?" The crystal clarity of Carreen's word cut through all other sounds and voices.

He turned to see her with a slight glow.

"FORGIVEN!" Matthew yelled.

Before the word was out of his mouth, the scene changed again to another hurt he had suffered.

Matthew could feel her smiling at him as he looked around for her and yelled his reply before she asked. "Forgiven!"

His declaration had an immediate impact on Carreen's glow.

Scene after scene came in rapid fire as he continued his reply. Matthew could no longer look at the blinding likeness of Carreen, but he was content watching the Accuser brace for another blow as his words hit hard and true. Matthew wore her glow as a coat and felt her smile as the scenes continued to flash by.

He hardly noticed the Accuser exit. The scenes started to slow, and when they stopped he saw someone positioned with his back to him. Automatically, Matthew started to say "for—."The rest of the word caught in his mouth. He was looking at himself. As the man Matthew once was turned to face him, he started to cry.

The man Matthew once was reached out and touched his shoulder as the new Matthew recoiled. "You wasted my whole life!"

Then he felt Carreen's hand grasp his fingers. He looked at her as she mouthed the word.

"How can I? I still shudder when I think of how close I came to—"

"He's changed."

Matthew fell to his knees, and the ground changed below him from the polished tile of the restaurant to dried earth.

"Well?"

Matthew felt the word well up in him as he let out the smallest of whispers pass out of his mouth. "Forgiven."

"It is finished!" the reply came back, shattering Matthew's words.

At that moment, the ground began to shake as rocks split in two. People were running everywhere. Matthew ran to the cross, fell at the base, and wrapped his arms around it. It was his turn not to care about the crowd, not to care about time, not to care about what others thought, but just to care about Jesus.

"Check and make sure that he's dead."

Matthew heard the soldiers standing around him but didn't care. He could hear one of them picking up a spear. He looked up and saw the spear pierce Jesus' side. He didn't care that blood and water was everywhere—he wasn't going to leave his friend. He stood up and put his arms around Jesus' feet and cried.

Chapter 27 – Response Coma

Jane stared at the monitor as the numbers refreshed every three seconds. Doctor Gray was right. The "bolt," as he called it, gave her a sense of comfort. The numbers washed over her like the waves at the beach.

Sometimes the number would start to climb. She could feel her pulse and breathing quicken, riding the wave as it would crest, then fall, finding herself carried away in the pool of smaller numbers. In the past two days the numbers had never peaked in the danger zone. Now they just carried her in the tranquil sea of numb.

In the beginning she thought the numbers would continue to rise, but they didn't. With each rise there would be a fall.

While in this sea of numb she would drift back and forth, peacefully detached, over the events that recently rocked her world until she was hit with that word, "bolt."

Earlier she and Daniel saw Matthew for just a few minutes. Enough time for a quick prayer and "I love you" and he was gone again, wheeled down the corridor for the Bolt procedure.

Matthew stayed in recovery until 1:00 a.m., when they transferred him to ICU so he could be monitored around the clock. The first seventy-two hours were critical; after that the threat of swelling will have passed.

There was still a small group of six that moved from emergency to the ICU waiting room. Pastor Brightwell and his wife finally convinced Daniel to come home with them. Jane was unable to leave Matthew's side for more than a few minutes. The hospital placed a cot in his room for her to get some rest.

Later that morning was when everything stopped. It happened when Doctor Gray was making his rounds.

Doctor Gray picked up Matthew's chart. "Looks like Matthew had a good night. I'll need him for a few minutes. One of the nurses will come and get you when I'm finished."

Jane grabbed a bag of corn chips from the vending machine just down the hall from the ICU waiting room and headed outside for just few minutes to get a little fresh air.

Daniel got up early so Pastor Brightwell could drop him off at the hospital on his way to the church. As they drove through the parking lot he noticed his mom sitting on a bench next to the hospital entrance.

She waved as they approached and walked over to the driver's side as they stopped. Pastor put the car in park and got out to give Jane a hug. "Any change?"

"No change, but he had a good night. Doctor Gray is with him now."

"Do you need me to stay?"

"No, we're fine. Thanks for giving Daniel a break."

"Our pleasure. He's a great kid. I'll drop by later this afternoon."

Jane walked over to Daniel and embraced him. "Glad you're back."

"Talk to dad yet?"

"No, but his numbers are good. Doctor Gray is checking him out. His body is probably trying to make up for all of those short nights."

"I got you a bagel," Daniel said as he started to spread cream cheese on one of the slices.

"Thanks, hon. He looks better today."

"Pastor said he would call the travel agency. I hope it's okay."

Jane just nodded as a tear dropped on her bagel. "We'll go next year."

"He'll drop by later this afternoon. I got his cell in case we need him."

"Yeah he told me. He's a good man," she said, staring into space. "Seems like a different lifetime."

Jane was able to take a few bites when the nurse came to get them. She took a small sip of iced tea and followed Daniel into the ICU.

Doctor Gray smiled as they entered Matthew's room. "He's done real well for his first twenty-four hours."

"So when's sleeping beauty going to wake up? Mom's already tried the kissing thing," Daniel said.

Jane blushed. "Daniel."

Doctor Gray didn't laugh. "Those micro tears still worry me. We'll be taking more MRIs this afternoon. It's hard to say how long he'll be in a—"

Jane's head seemed to fill with water when he said the word: "C o m a."

Her response seemed just as muffled and slurred when she said it back.   "*C o m a?*"

Doctor Gray's words floated through her memory. "*C o u l d   b e   d a y s s s,   c o u l d   b e   m o n t h s s s.*"

For now she floated through waves of numbers as she cast a lifeline to her husband. "*M a t t h e w   c o m e   b a c k   to   me.   D a n i e l   n e e d s   y o u.   I   n e e d   y o u...*"

R e s p o n s e.... C o m a.

Chapter 28 – Feeling Shiny

He could hear the wind as it started to blow and with it, the Carpenter's voice echoing in his ears: "The wind here is a little different."

Matthew stood to face the wind and closed his eyes. It shot through him, this time with fire, consuming him, burning all the anger, selfishness, shame, and pride. As the wind died down, he found himself on his knees inside his home. It was quiet now, and peaceful. He was touching his healed life just like the leper whose hand felt smoothness in the once diseased face. Matthew felt goodness in his soul, which had once been corrupted and riddled with sin. He could feel that his face was shining. He could still remember all the things he had done, but it was like that Matthew no longer existed. Just this cleaned up, shiny one.

Matthew was sitting there smiling at the thoughts going through his mind when he heard a knock at the door. *That was odd.* Who would be knocking at my door? Matthew was excited and raced to the door and opened it. There in the doorway stood his carpenter friend Jesus, decked out in a glowing robe and grinning from ear to ear.

"Jesus!" Matthew exclaimed as he fell at his feet. "I was so blind, I—"

"I'm just glad you opened the door," Jesus said as he touched Matthew's shoulder and walked inside.

Matthew stood up and followed Jesus inside. "What? You're just glad I opened the door?"

"Yeah, I'm just glad you opened the door. Don't worry— someday you'll get it and really like it."

Matthew just shook his head as he motioned for Jesus to have a seat.

As he sat down he raised his eyebrow. "So Matthew, how does it feel to be shiny?"

Now Matthew was grinning. "It feels free… really free. Not like a free *from* something but a free *to* something. I don't feel bad about myself anymore; I don't really understand, but I know I belong."

"Matthew," Jesus went on to explain. "It wasn't about your corruptness but about God's holiness and love. God's plan was always for you to belong, but freedom comes at a price."

"And you were that price."

"You were worth it, Matthew."

"Not me by myself."

"Yes, just you by yourself."

"But how about Daniel, Jane, or Anne?"

"They are all worth it."

"I would never have thought I was worth much, but I have never seen myself like this," Matthew said, grinning from ear to ear.

"The world doesn't want you to see yourself like this. That way, you believe and fall into all kind of traps and trust lies as truth. God has always wanted you to be what he created you to be, but sin would blind you and then lead you down the wrong path. Pride and shame will take you like a pig to the slaughter. They will puff you up so that even God should be answerable to you, and then they will slam you down so that nothing can help the fool you have become. They want you to think of yourself as more than you are or less that what you are. As long as you do not see who you really are, they have you."

"That's why something that is so simple is really so hard," said Matthew as the truth hit him. "I mean… like the ABCs: admit, believe, and confess. To do it, you must ignore the laughing and taunting of pride and shame as you admit that you're a sinner, believe in Jesus, and confess your sins and commit your life to God. Thank you for letting me get to know you before revealing to me who you are."

"It's been my pleasure, Matthew Six."

Chapter 29 - Roses

"Jane, there's a Martha Elliot in the waiting room here to see Matthew. Should I let her in?"

"That's okay, I'll go get her. She's the one who found Matthew."

Jane walked down the hall and hit the button to open the large double doors.

Daniel was on the other side, talking to a woman who was holding a bouquet of flowers. "I know they are beautiful, but you can't."

"The young lady at the hospital florist looked it up for me. Doctor Peterson is allowed to have them."

"Martha."

"Mrs. Peterson." Martha walked through the large double doors with a perplexed Daniel in tow. "These are for you."

"Sorry, mom, I tried to…"

Jane looked at Daniel with her we'll-talk-later eyebrow in high gear. "It's okay, Daniel."

She took them from Martha like they were fine china and cradled them in her arms. "They are beautiful, Martha," she said as she closed her eyes and took in the fragrance. "My favorites" was all she could say as a few tears fell on the roses.

"Are you okay, Mrs. Peterson?"

"Yes, they are very special. Thank you, and please call me Jane. How are you doing, Martha?"

"The doctors gave me something. It helps when I start to think too much about it."

"You did a wonderful thing for us." Jane carefully handed the roses to Daniel, then she gave Martha a hug.

As they walked toward Matthew's room, Jane introduced the nurses she knew to Martha, the hero who saved her husband.

They entered Matthew's room to the soft sounds of a music CD with the humming of machines in the background.

"He's connected to a lot of stuff," Daniel said, breaking the silence.

"Is he okay?" Martha asked.

"All of his vitals are stable, and there's been no swelling, thank God. We've really been feeling everyone's prayers."

"What's that thing," she said, pointing to the bolt.

"It's a Bolt; it monitors the pressure in his brain. That's the number right there on the monitor. Dad's pressure's never been in the danger zone."

Jane took Martha's hand and brought her closer. "They said he might be able to hear us." She bent over Matthew and caressed his forehead, running her fingers through his sweaty hair. "Matthew, Matthew honey? It's Jane. I'm here with Daniel and someone very special. It's Martha from work. She's the one that found you."

"You're looking good, Doctor Peterson," Martha said, trying to smile.

Jane gave her two thumbs up.

"We all miss you a lot. Don't tell Anne I told you, but she still thinks you planned the fire alarm as a farewell surprise."

Terri one of the nurses taking care of Matthew entered the room. "Wow, what a beautiful bouquet of roses."

They all turned to see her admiring the roses Daniel was holding.

"We have a large vase in the storage room. I'll go get it so we can get those beauties in water."

"Thanks, Terri," Jane said. "Before you go, I would like to introduce you to the angel who saved my husband. Terri this is Martha. Martha, Terri."

Terri looked down at Martha's shoes. "And she's a sharp dresser, too."

Martha blushed, enjoying the compliment.

"When I get back you can tell me where you shop, and you can be my hero, too."

Martha lit up. "Shopping… sure. Let me help you get that vase."

Daniel gave his mother a puzzled look as the laughter of the two women faded down the hall.

Jane smiled. "A couple more compliments like that and Martha won't need 'a little something' from the doctors anymore."

Daniel changed the subject. "I thought you didn't like roses."

"I never said that I didn't like roses. They are, and have always been, my absolute favorite."

"But dad said."

"Dad said no roses; I know. I asked him not to buy me roses."

"What?"

Jane placed her hand on Daniel's shoulder. "I know it's hard to understand. They are so special to me that I only allow myself to have them one day a year. At noon I buy the roses and spend the afternoon in the park with my Bible and diary. People passing by will mention how beautiful the roses are."

Daniel saw a sad longing on his mother's face that he had seen only on his dad's face before. He held his mom close. "It's okay; you don't have to explain."

"One by one, I give them away until there's only one left, the most beautiful one. I walk around inhaling the scent until twilight. Then I…"

Daniel could feel his mother sobbing quietly as he held her.

"I hold tight on the stem and pull off the rose and place the rose in a small stream and watch as it drifts out of sight. Then I sit back and listen to the nature all around me as I watch the stars come out and look for the one that is mine."

"Doesn't it cut your hand?"

"Yes it does, Daniel. For days it will remind me of the pain of being apart. As it heals it reminds me that the pain won't always be there because someday we will be together."

"Whoa… that's amazing, Mom."

"Yes it is, son. Yes it is".

Chapter 30 - Dad

"Rose, he's here!"

"I know," came the reply from the young redhead as she smiled an I'm-glad-but-I'm-scared-smile.

"Like you always tell me, the Father always has a way of surprising us. Things seem to take so long, and then all of a sudden what we've waited and prayed for is here."

Her eyes met his and just drank in the love for a long moment, and they started to sparkle in return. "I do always say that, don't I?"

"Yes you do," he replied. His fiery eyes returned her gaze.

"A long time ago I knew just what to say, just what to ask, but now I'm not so sure. He has changed so much, but I do so want to see him," she said, biting on her lower lip and knowing Marcus would glance down just for a moment, breaking his gaze.

He shook his head and smiled. "Why don't you meet him in the garden? The beauty and the music will transcend the words you cannot say."

"Of course, you're right, Marcus," said Rose as she punched his stomach and turned to go.

"I'm always right when it comes to someone else, just like you, Rose," shouted Marcus, cupping his hands to his mouth.

"Pray for me!" she said as she looked back and then took off across the meadow. As Rose approached, she could hear the music. She stopped and let the melody surround her. She always enjoyed listening to and feeling someone else's song. Each one was always so unique and special. Matthew's song was different in that somehow parts of it were the same as another song… hers.

She could see him now with his eyes closed, wrapped up in the song. As he started into a piece Rose knew as hers, she joined it.

Together they played their song. At one point Matthew noticed something was different; he opened his eyes and saw her. Startled, he stopped.

Rose smiled. "Hi, I'm Rose"

"My name is Matthew." Matthew held out his hand.

She took his hand in both of hers and stared into his face.

"Rose is such a beautiful name. My wife always liked it," said Matthew, smiling.

"That's why I chose it, Dad." Rose held tightly to his hand.

The words shot through him as he fell to his knees. "I'm sorry... we didn't... I didn't." Then he started to cry.

Rose let go of his hand a put her arms around his head and drew him close. "Dad." The word she had longed to say felt good on her lips. "I love you." He cried as she held him close and kept saying over and over again, "I love you, Dad. Dad, your little girl loves you. Dad, I've been fine. I... missed you... longed for you. I just wanted to call you Dad and..." At this, Rose started to cry.

It was Matthew's turn to hold Rose close and talk to her through his tears. "It's ok, Daddy's here. I'm sorry... I made so many wrong choices. God is so good... moment by moment, he is restoring things I had destroyed. Oh Rose, God is so good to give you back to me. My Rose. You know you look a lot like your mother. You don't know what this will mean to her. A dark, sad, and lonely place will be turned into a place of joy and happiness."

Rose looked deep into Matthew's eyes. "Mom already knows I'm here. We are all here. Every child makes it here and each one longs to be reunited. My mom is very special. She sends me a rose every year."

"What?"

"Yes. She turned a curse into a blessing. Hurt turned around can become healing. Every time I get a rose, heaven cheers."

Matthew smiled. "She has come a long way."

"Dad?" Rose said, looking up into his eyes.

"Yes, Rose." Matthew caressed her hair in his hand.

"There's something I always wanted to do," she said, as a smile came over her face. "I always wanted to run into your arms and you would pick me up and throw me in the air."

He looked Rose over. She was almost as tall as he was. "Honey, I'm not sure I could…"

As he spoke she grew younger right before his eyes. "You're not sure you could what?" she said with the giggle of the two-year-old she had become. "Come on Daddy, catch me." With that, she threw herself into his arms.

He threw her up in the air, and she giggled. "Do it again, Daddy. Do it again!" He picked her up to do it again, and a new song started from the ashes of the old. He held her by the waist above his head, and she spread out her arms like an airplane. As he ran through the meadow, she flew over his head. Then he grabbed one arm and one foot and twirled his little Rose around and around till they both got dizzy and ended up in a laughing heap on the ground.

"Daddy?" Rose asked, laying down and looking up into the sky.

"Yes, Rose," Matthew replied as he lay beside his little girl, studying her beautiful little face and flowing red hair.

"Why do people want things that aren't real?"

"Well, they don't always know that the things they want aren't real."

"But they know they won't last, don't they?" Rose asked.

"Yes, most of the time they know that things won't last. Most people think nothing will last."

"Nothing?" she said.

"Nothing." He shook his head. "They think that when they die, that's it. Ashes to ashes, dust to dust."

"What about the soul?" Rose inquired.

"If they can't see it, they don't believe it."

"What do you mean they can't see it?"

"Rose, they can't see someone's soul."

"They can't?" said Rose, shaking her head.

"No, they can't, sweetie."

Rose stood up with her hands on her hips, still the little girl. "But Daddy!" she said, trying on her best grownup face. "If they can't see someone's soul, then how can they know who they really are?"

Matthew couldn't resist. He stood, up grabbed Rose's hands, and started to twirl her around and around. "You can't tell who someone really is, sweetie—only what they show you. The sad truth is that many times they don't even show themselves. They believe what their head tells them, not their heart."

Rose started to giggle and shook her head. "That is silly!"

Matthew stopped and tried hard not to laugh. "No it's not."

"Yes it is. It's silly, silly, silly…" she shouted, running away.

"No it's not," cried Matthew as he tried to catch her.

"Yes it is!" Rose howled as her father closed in.

"No it's not." Matthew bellowed triumphantly as he grabbed Rose around the waist and started to tickle her.

"It isss..stiillll… sss..iillll…yyyy," she shrieked through the laughter.

Matthew fell to his knees and wrapped his arms around her squirmy little body, feeling her laughter as he put his head on her shoulder and whispered into her ear, "I love you, Rose."

"I love you, Daddy," came the reply. He closed his eyes to swim in the words as tears, happy, content tears, flowed down his face.

"Daddy?"

"Yes, Rose."

"I still think it's silly," she said, her body starting to shake. "It… does explain… a lot!"

"What? What do you mean, it explains a lot?" Matthew said. He twirled her around to face him.

"Think about it, Dad. It is really silly, and it does explain a lot, like the way you used to squeeze the toothpaste," she said, smiling.

"I guess the toothpaste was pretty silly," Matthew said, shaking his head and smiling at the thought.

"Pretty, pretty silly!" As Rose spoke, she grew back into the young lady he had first seen. "You would squeeze the tube from the middle in defiance and then put the lid on and squeeze it from the end so you wouldn't get in trouble."

"Yes, I guess that was silly," Matthew said. The smile on his face looked like he had been caught with his hand in the cookie jar.

"You guess? I always thought that was hilarious because you were so serious about getting your way. You only did it for twenty years." Now Rose was looking straight at her father with her eyebrows raised. "And how about the car, young man? Was that not silly?"

Matthew was trying to hold his lips together as his cheeks expanded with the laughter that was trying to escape. "Yes ma'am!" he agreed with an explosion of laughter.

Now she was on him, tickling him for all she was worth. "Yes ma'am, what?"

"Yeesss... Maaa'aa..mm it... was... ssiiiilllyyy." he stuttered through the laughter and tears.

"Now say Rose is right."

"What?"

"Rose is right! Say it. Come on, say it."

"Don't do it," called the voice of a large man running toward them from the other end of the meadow.

"Don't listen to him. Say it—Rose is right!"

"Don't do it," boomed the man's voice as he got closer.

"Who is that?" Matthew said as he tried to turn around.

"Nobody," Rose said as she grabbed his head with both hands and forced him to look into her eyes. "Say it and I'll tell you."

"Ok, Rose is right," Matthew said just as a hand touched his shoulder.

"Noooo!" Marcus' voice was filled with dread as he rushed by, falling down, but it was too late—Rose had gotten what she wanted.

Rose released her dad, with a satisfied my-job-is-done-here smile. "Dad, I'd like you to meet Marcus. Marcus this is my Dad. Dad, you and Marcus have something in common. You both know a great truth: Rose is right."

"Right," echoed Jesus.

Now it was Marcus's and Matthew's turn to laugh as they saw the surprise on Rose's face. Her smile had changed to a hand-caught-in-the-cookie-jar smile as Jesus put his arm around her neck and gave her his big-brother, we've-had-this-talk-before smile.

"So Marcus, how's the book coming?" asked Jesus as he and Rose sat down facing the two men.

"Book? Well, I… I think I'm going to write about a missionary to the cannibals in the Andes, or maybe the martyrs in France, or the—"

"Marcus, you have a great story of your own. Why don't you start with your wonderful story?" Jesus said.

"Who I was is already out there for anyone who wants to see it."

"They may know what happened, but they can't know the real you unless you tell them. Marcus, trust me—you have a great story. Men will hear it and give glory to God."

"You know that's all I want," Marcus said. "To give glory to God. I want everyone to know how powerful and mighty God is, but they already know that."

"Marcus," Jesus interrupted. "Have they seen God through your eyes?"

"No, I guess not."

"Marcus, what do you know about Matthew?"

"A lot. Matthew has a great story, and he never hurt any Christians."

"A great story… How could you say I have a great story?" Matthew said to Marcus. "Man lives his whole life for himself and gives his last two seconds to God. Not much of a story…Hey… how did you know about me?"

"Everyone kno—" Marcus started to reply.

"Matthew and Marcus," Jesus interrupted. "Every story about a sinner set free is great. Each one is in the 'Book of Life' for all to see."

"My story… my life is in a book for all to see," Matthew pondered and shook his head.

"Not exactly," replied Jesus. "The Book of Life contains the story of each person's life but not each person's story."

"But what if I don't want everyone to know what I did? There is so much I'm ashamed of," replied Matthew.

"You have nothing to be ashamed of," Rose said. She got up from where she was and sat next to her father.

"Rose is right," Jesus said, then shook his head as they all started to laugh. "Each believer's story has been covered by grace. Story after story unlocks the wonder of God's love toward man, telling just how precious each soul is to him and how far he went to redeem it."

"So all of the things people would be ashamed of have been removed," Matthew replied. He smiled in relief.

"For the believer," Jesus said. Tears started forming in his eyes as he repeated, "For the believer."

Rose moved to Jesus and held his face between her soft gentle hands. As she stared into his eyes, tears formed in her own. She picked up where Jesus left off. "The unbeliever doesn't know grace and without grace, each and every transgression will be seen condemning the unbeliever to an eternity in hell."

At this, Jesus' tears flowed down this face as he started to shake his head. Still holding his face between her hands, Rose said, "I know. I know it was never meant for them."

Without taking her eyes off Jesus, she told them eternity's story.

Chapter 31 – Story of Man

Before time but after eternity began, God created the heavenly host. Among them was one who was the model of perfection, full of wisdom, and perfect in beauty. Lucifer was an anointed guardian angel, ordained on the holy mountain of God, adorned with every precious stone. He worshiped God in front of His throne and was over one-third of the heavenly host. This angel was blameless from the day he was created until his heart became proud. He tried to elevate himself and take over the throne of God for himself. God removed Lucifer from his position, and one-third of the angels fell joining Satan in his rebellion. God prepared hell for Satan and his demons.

God created the Heavens and the Earth and all living creatures. Then he created man and woman in his own image, molding them from the dust of the earth and breathing his own breath of life into them. He placed them in a beautiful garden, supplying all their needs. God walked with them. He gave them language and enjoyed watching them explore and name all of his creation. There was only one rule, one simple rule: Do not to eat of the tree of Knowledge of Good and Evil. He told them they must never eat of it. The day they would eat of it, they would surely die.

Satan despised man. Wasn't it he who had been with God before they even existed? Didn't God make him perfect in every way? And now he was being replaced by beings who were bound by time and space, beings who had temporary bodies made out of dust. Satan could hear all of heaven laughing. *Oh how the mighty have fallen.*

Through his consuming hatred of God and man, Satan devised a plan—a plan of deception, a plan of greed, a plan of death. He would cloak deception in knowledge, greed in equality, and death in life. He knew the perfect tool to unlock his treasures: pride. If it was good enough for the perfect one, it would surely be good enough for these worms. Besides, it would be like placing his own mark inside them, driving a wedge between God and man.

Satan patiently planted seeds, seeds of doubt and equality. This was done well before the tree of Knowledge of Good and Evil had any fruit. The day the buds flowered, it started.

"Come look at these flowers," called the deceiver. "There are none like them in the entire garden."

"They are beautiful," the woman said admiringly with the man at her side. "But we are not to touch this tree or its fruit."

"I've heard of that rule; I wonder why he made it. They are so beautiful." Satan smiled to himself. A little deception coated in truth, such a tasty morsel.

"Are we allowed to look upon the tree? I wouldn't want to do anything wrong."

This is just too… eeassssy, he hissed to himself.

"God didn't say… I'm sure it would be okay. It is so beautiful, and the flowers smell so sweet," said the woman.

"*Seeeee youuuu tomorrow*," said Satan as he left to watch from a distance.

Day after day they met, marveling at the tree and the fruit that started to form. Day after day the seeds were watered. "Well, I've got to go. I wonder why he made that rule." Satan would wonder aloud for her to hear.

Then one day the fruit was ready, and so was he. This day, instead of admiring the tree and its fruit, he sat silent. This silence screamed at the woman, baiting her.

"What's wrong? You're so quiet," said the woman with the man at her side.

"It's just, well, I shouldn't," said the deceiver as he looked at the ground.

"What is it? You can tell us. We are your friends," they said in unison.

He heard the silence of heaven as he set the hook: "I found out why God doesn't want you to eat the fruit." He didn't even wait for their reply. "You will not die when you eat from the tree. God knows once you eat of it your eyes will be opened, and you will be like God, knowing good and evil. You will have wisdom." He excused himself, "Well I've got to go."

For the next few days he watched in delight as they fought the temptation. Then one day it happened. The woman reached up and quickly took a bite and smiled with delight as the juice ran down her chin. She gave it to her husband, and he quickly devoured it as she grabbed another.

Satan had tempted them to be like God and decide for themselves what is good and what is evil, causing the fall of man and giving the deceiver dominion over their world. Worst of all, the deception had separated man from God.

God also had a plan, a plan that would battle pride with humility and hatred with love. He sent his only son to pay with his life the price needed to redeem man from sin. This salvation would restore man's relationship to God if he would only humble himself and accept it and turn to God.

When each life is shown, three things will be revealed. The first will be God's Truth, Love, and Mercy toward man. The second will be Satan's Deception, Hate, and Cruelty. The Third will be who we believed. If we accepted God's gift, paid for by his son, and put our trust in God we will go to heaven. If not, we go to hell.

Once in hell, Satan will be given free rein to torment those who believed his lies. Fire and worms will consume them, but they will not die.

Many don't believe it. This is just what Satan wants. He longs to torment the Creator's creation.

It is each man's choice.

Chapter 32 – Afraid of the Dark

Jesus placed his hands around Rose's hands and mouthed the words "thank you" to Rose, then drew them down to his chest, placing her hands over his heart. Turning to Marcus, he said, "Would you tell your story, Marcus? It really is a great story."

Marcus thought for a moment, staring at the ground. "Where do I begin?"

"Start with the fear. Do you remember the fear?" asked Jesus.

"The fear," Marcus said softy to himself. Then, looking up at Jesus, "Yes, I remember as if it just happened. It's strange... I remember it so well, but it no longer holds me." Glancing down, he said, "The fear... yes that's it." Gazing up at Jesus again, "That's where it all started, isn't it?"

"Yes it was, Marcus." Jesus smiled.

"It's a funny thing, fear." Marcus gave out a sad, nervous laugh. "It will drive you wherever it wants to go and render you helpless, all the time consuming your soul. I was afraid of the dark."

It was a strange sight—a huge, strong, muscular man saying he was afraid of the dark, but they didn't laugh. They were hooked and wanted more.

"Well?" encouraged Matthew after a few moments had passed.

Marcus looked up and started his story...

Like I was saying, I was afraid of the dark. I was the youngest of six boys born to the house of Lucian, a Roman Centurion, servant of his Excellency Claudius, Emperor of Rome. We lived in a large house on a small farm away from the cities and villages. When my brothers wanted to go exploring and didn't want me to tag along, they would lock me in the cellar. I didn't mind too much because there was much exploring a young man could do with a bunch of old trunks and broken down tools.

One day, shortly after I turned six, my brothers locked me in the cellar, but this time they didn't return until late. As the last rays of light shot through the opening far above the stairwell, the room started to change. The heavy beams above me turned red. Shadows moved between the boards and started to moan as the wind whistled through the cracks. I yelled and screamed, the sounds bouncing off the walls and mocking me with my own cries. My parents were away on a trip and my brothers were nowhere to be found. I was alone.

The red turned slowly to gray. The gray turned black, and the cellar continued to creak and moan as if from old age. Then it happened. Someone blew out the sound as if it were a candle. I could feel my heart pounding in my chest, and I felt someone… or *something* evil in the room. I made my way to the corner and sat down facing the empty darkness. Fear gripped me with its icy talons. I felt like I was being lifted through the blackness high into the inky night, being held there in space for the gods to laugh at, a toy for the gods to play with. They enjoyed seeing my fear until they got bored.

The laughing stopped, and they said in unison, in a flat, cold voice, "Let him fall."

I felt myself falling faster and faster. I tried to scream but was mute with terror. I tried to move but was paralyzed with dread. I felt the bottom rushing up toward me. I had to break free. Then in one mighty move I took a deep breath and broke free from my bondage. I started to yell as I felt myself crash into the ground.

Sound came back in a rush as I heard someone's screams mingled with my own. My arm was on fire. This all happened in an instant. I opened my eyes to find myself on the floor of my room with my mother screaming for someone to get the oil. I jumped up off of the burning ground and started to run through the house, screaming, holding my arm. One of my brothers grabbed me from behind, and another one poured oil on my red, swollen arm.

Once I calmed down, my mother told me that my brothers had found me on the floor of the cellar. My clothes were soaked with sweat, and I was burning up. They carried me into the house but couldn't get me to wake up. A spider had bitten me. Four days I had been fighting, my body rigid as a board. Then all at once I start yelling and threw my arms up, knocking over a bowl of boiling water on my arm. My mother was using the hot water to clean the wound, hoping it would draw out the poison.

For almost a month I repeated the same dream, waking everyone as I screamed and fell on the ground. The first week my mother would rush to my side to wipe the cold sweat from my face and back. Then my father told her to let me be—it was time to grow up. Night after night I felt the fear, heard the laughter, and was helpless as my terror ended with shrieks of horror and me throwing myself on the floor. I would lay there shaking the rest of the night, my only comfort coming from my mother's muffled cries from the other side of the house.

It was now late in the year, soon to be winter, so there was little time to relax and feel sorry for myself. My father would slap me on the back and say, "The men of the house of Lucian eat fear for breakfast and feed it to others for lunch. Take heart, Marcus—one day, fear will run from you and you will hunt it down like the coward it is. Now we have work to do. Winter will soon be upon us. It cares not for fear or laughter."

I didn't mind winter because father was home. Spring would come all too soon, and father would leave, taking his place with the Third Legion. This spring my oldest brother Sidonius would go with him. During the winter, my father would tell of the last year's adventures, stories of the honor and glory of Rome and the men who fought for her.

My nightmare no longer plagued me and seemed like it was gone forever, but it came back when my father left that spring. I remembered what he told me, and I would hit myself on the side of the head and say, "The men of the house of Lucian eat fear for breakfast and feed it to others for lunch. Take heart, Marcus—one day, fear will run from you and you will hunt it down like the coward it is." It seemed to help. After a few days the nightmares stopped.

Every chance we got, my brothers and I practiced the art of battle so that someday we too could go with our father. With so many older brothers, I grew up tough. When they dared me to do something, I would do it, until one day they wanted me to go into the cellar. When I said "no," they made a big mistake; they started to laugh at me until they saw the demon in my eyes. Then they ran away as I went wild, but they didn't run soon enough. I started hitting, scratching, and biting everything I could get my hands on. That day they had a small taste of the fear I'd been living with.

The years went by, and one by one my brothers left in the spring. Now they were spread across the vast Roman Empire. From Great Britain to North Africa they fought for the empire. By my sixteenth year I was bigger than all my brothers and had learned to turn my fear into rage, and rage into power. My love was power. The more I got, the more I wanted. I would strap an old wagon wheel on my back and carry it around all day just to feel the power in my limbs. I longed for my first battle so I could crush my enemy and feel my power over them.

I could tell my father was worried. Ever since Nero became emperor, he would tell me, "Power without honor shows weakness." He wouldn't say it, but the Rome he loved was changing. Honor had been replaced with disgrace. He told me next year's campaign would be his last.

That winter when he told me stories of last year's battles, he seemed different. He didn't give one battle cry or cut the air with his invisible sword. Now it was just him and me, with mother baking in the other room. He sat in his big chair telling his stories as if he were daydreaming, talking to the air. When I was younger I sat on the edge of my seat, my heart aflame. Now I was hardly paying any attention.

"Do you remember Justin of Sardinia?" he asked, bringing me back from my thoughts.

I nodded; Justin had been the captain of the garrison my father was assigned to for his first three campaigns. Justin had visited a few times when I was young. I would ride on his back, standing taller than all of my brothers. Justin and I would defend the Empire from these pagan hoards. Through the years, I had heard of the great exploits of Justin. I sat up waiting to hear of another great story of Justin.

My father just stared into my eyes, studying my face. "Justin is gone, son."

His words shot through me. "How?" was all I could say.

"Part of a wall had fallen on him, and he was bleeding to death from the inside. In his last hours, he called for me. He wanted to release me from my vow."

"Vow?" I interrupted.

"Yes, Justin had sworn me to a vow never to tell... until now..." My father looked off in the distance, then told me of the vow he had made to Justin years before. A vow to never repeat a story Justin had told him. For years Justin had been part of a special group of centurions assigned to Pontius Pilate to keep the peace in Palestine during the times of the Jewish festivals. I know of none braver than my father, but for the first time, I saw fear in his eyes when he told me the story.

Chapter 33 – Becoming a Soldier

After a long pause Matthew broke the silence. "Well aren't you going to tell us the story of Justin?"

Marcus looked flustered. "It's really Justin's story. I'm just not sure. I…"

Jesus put his hand on Marcus's shoulder. "It's okay to tell whatever you're comfortable with."

"You sure it's okay?"

"Yes, Marcus, I'm sure."

"Is it okay with you, Matthew?"

"I am curious, but yes, it's okay, as long as you introduce me to Justin."

Marcus smiled. "I'd be glad to. Now where was I?"

"The last winter with your father," Jesus said.

Marcus closed his eyes and was transported to another time.

* * *

That winter was rough, and I was glad. The hard work made for dreamless nights, and spring came quickly. After all these years I would be joining my father in battle. Winter came and went and with it the gloom that had been planted in my father's heart. Early one spring morning he woke me while it was still dark.

"Are you going to sleep all day, soldier?!" he barked. As I quickly dressed, he laid out the plan. My father was back. "Today we go on reconnaissance mission. You up for it?"

"Yes, sir. I've been waiting my whole life for it, sir." I wanted to hug him but instead I gave him an I-am-so-proud-to-be-your-son smile.

He looked at me for just a moment and then barked, "Wipe that smile off your face, solider," while he flashed an I-am-so-proud-of-you-son grin. That's my dad.

Somehow I finished getting dressed. That was one of the greatest days of my life. I felt like I became a man that day. Almost every day for the next month we did something to prepare me for life as a soldier. At least that's what I thought.

My first year as a soldier was not what I had expected. Now I knew why my brothers laughed when I would talk about the exploits of my first year. That year I made camp, broke down camp, made camp, broke camp, made camp, and broke down camp. When I wasn't making or breaking camp I dug the latrine and took care of the laundry.

During the last week of that year's campaign the first year's soldiers were chosen to become part of one of the many garrisons. Once chosen, I would live with the garrison for the next five years. Those who were not chosen would return home just to live their first year over again. Because of my size, and I think my father, I was the first man chosen.

Five days later I said good-bye to my father. He gave me a cloth from my mother and told me to treasure it. Then he hit me on the shoulder, almost knocking me down.

"Make the house of Lucian proud," he said, then turned to leave. He took a few steps and looked back at me and said almost in a whisper, "Be well my son." And then he was gone.

I just stood there. "Be well father," I said, knowing he could not hear. I watched as he disappeared beyond the crest of the hill. He was gone and I started to feel alone, but then I noticed I was holding something: the cloth from my mother. I held it up to my face and closed my eyes. I was home and she was nearby; the cloth smelled of her.

Chapter 34 - Power

Garrison life was not much different than living with five older brothers. You even have a captain for a father. Mothers, on the other hand, could not be replaced. I found out many of the soldiers both young and old had a piece of cloth from their mother or wife. That winter I learned to fight, but it wasn't until that spring when we marched north that I found out what it was like to kill a man. I felt the power of taking another man's life. I saw the surprise in their eyes as death found them at the tip of my sword, followed by the fear, the fear that gave me power.

My thirst for power grew every time I overpowered someone. I could see the fear in their eyes and hear my father's voice: "The men of the house of Lucian eat fear for breakfast and feed it to others for lunch." I was now the master of fear. Sure, I heard the stories that Rome was becoming weak, but I didn't care because I was growing strong.

Because of my fierceness in battle I was reassigned to the city of Rome. I was to be groomed to become a gladiator. The next two years I trained with all kind of weapons and learned from the biggest and best of Rome. My first battle as a gladiator, I felt so much power as we reenacted one of Rome's famous battles. We were outnumbered two to one, but they didn't have a chance. They had their choice of weapons, many of them even bigger than we were, but we worked as a well-oiled machine. I didn't have time to stare in the eyes of the first two, but the third was my last, and I enjoyed seeing the fear overcome that huge hulk as the crowd determined his fate. When the cheer went up and the signal was given, I felt more power than ever as the fear in his eyes became that familiar glassy stare I had seen so often.

The next six months we reenacted many of Rome's victories. Once in a while a Gladiator would fall, but I didn't care. All I cared about was me. We were told that in the next few weeks the games would change. We would be fighting Pagan enemies of Rome. These enemies of Rome would not bow to Caesar and threatened Rome's power. I was ready to show them what real power was and watch as their power dissolved in fear. I heard the familiar cheers as we rushed out into the open arena ready to fight. We stopped in bewilderment. Before us was a small group of young and old men in a circle singing softly. Everyone laughed at the sight as the emperor gave the signal. These were the enemies of Rome?

"You saw the signal. Kill them!" demanded my commander.

Chapter 35 – Real Power

We grabbed them and pushed them to the ground. I heard the old man shout, "For us to live is Christ, and to die is gain!" just before he was silenced forever.

I picked up the young man I had hit, with the butt of my sword, so I could watch him die. As my sword ran him through and I lifted him off the ground, I heard him whisper through the pain, "Father, forgive him, for he knows not what he does."

In my anger at hearing those words I lifted him up as high as I could. As I did, instead of the surprise followed by fear, something happened that had never happened before. He smiled not only with his mouth but with his eyes. I brought him close, and the only fear I saw in his eyes was a reflection of my own.

Over the next few weeks we butchered hundreds, each one draining the power that once flowed through my veins. I could not fight this power that I saw in their eyes. I asked a soldier who brought in a group of these pagans where they were from.

"They are from that new sect they call 'The Way' that believe in the Christ," growled the guard.

"The Way?" I said to myself in horror, trying to remember some of the things my father had said about the sect.

My dream came back and with it all of its horror and humiliation, taunting me night after night. Day after day I lived another kind of horror. I watched as they threw these pagans into the arena to meet their death. They even started bringing in wild animals to tear them apart. My father was right—Rome was growing weak and losing its honor.

One day three women were thrown into the arena, but instead of tearing them apart, the animals attacked their owners and barely touched the women. Then we were sent out to finish the job. I could hardly jog to the center of the arena, and when I came face to face with one of the women, I felt like the blood drained from my face.

She seemed to glow as she smiled at me. "God loves you, Marcus. Be strong."

Unlike many of the others who showed some fear, she expressed joy. My arm shook as I started to pull my sword from its sheath. "How did you know my name?"

She smiled an I-know-something-you-don't-know smile. "Last night I saw you in my dream." Her smile turned to sadness. "I saw the terror in your eyes. True strength and peace can only come from God. It comes from love, not fear. Strike true and quickly, Marcus."

She grabbed the tip of my shaking sword and placed it against her chest. As I shook my head, she yelled, "Now!" I instinctively thrust the sword forward, then let go and fell to my knees as I heard a sharp cry ring out. I looked up and saw her raise her hands and smile. "Father, thank you for your peace and strength. Take me home." At that, she closed her eyes. She fell ever so gracefully to the ground.

Somehow I picked her up. She looked so peaceful with her eyes closed and a smile on her face. As I carried her, I felt the warmth leave her body, telling me she was truly gone. For the first time in my life I wished I could cry so I could give her one of my tears.

I paid the caretaker as I laid her on his cart. "She is special. Make certain she is well cared for."

I passed the cart and heard my name. "Marcus! Marcus!"

There was a group of prisoners in a holding cell waving and calling to me. "Marcus. Your name is Marcus isn't it. Petula said it was. Is it?"

I slowly approached the cell, looking down at the dirt floor and the blood still on my sandals. When I reached, the cell I looked up. "Was that her name? Petula?" The sadness in my face met the joy in theirs. "How can you have joy? She's gone."

An old man with a glint in his eye shook his head. "She's not gone, she is home. This life is but a mere breath, a blowing of the wind. She is now home with her Father and Lord."

I asked when her father died, and they all started to laugh. The old man explained, "Her Father and our Father is the Lord God, the one true God, who created all things. He loves us, and that includes you, Marcus."

I shook my head. "The gods don't love me. They torment me every night."

"Marcus," the old man said. "They are not gods at all. Tonight when they come, tell them you believe in the one true God and his son Jesus."

"Why would this one true God care about a Roman soldier who kills his people?" I said almost to myself.

"Why, he made you, Marcus. He knew everything about you before you were even born." The man looked up into my eyes, and I turned and walked away. "Talk to God, my son. Talk to him; you will see."

I quietly walked down the tunnels that led to my quarters. *Talk to God*, I thought to myself as I entered the large room.

Jason walked toward me and put a hand on my shoulder. "You had a beautiful one today, Marcus. What have they turned us into?"

I walked over to my cot and sat on the edge. "She knew my name, Jason. She knew my name."

Jason quickly grabbed a stool and sat down facing me. "What? How could she know? Did she ask someone? Did she use some kind of spell on you?"

I looked at Jason's feet. He had already washed the blood away. "She said she saw me in a dream, Jason."

"What else did she say?"

"She knew about my fear, my dream. Her name was Petula."

"How do you know that?"

"The old man in the holding cell told me. He also told me that Petula is home now. I don't really understand it. They say that all the gods we know and even the ones that torment me are not gods at all. They say there is only one true God who made everything. You know how most of them tell us God loves us?"

"Yes."

"They say that because he made all of us. He even sent his son Jesus. You've heard them speak about Jesus."

Jason nodded.

"They say this Jesus is God's only son, come to earth to die for us, to take our place, to pay the penalty for all the bad things we have done. My father told me a story about this Jesus."

Jason sat, shaking his head. "I've heard the stories; what a disgrace. Roman soldiers running from a few Jews."

I then told Jason about Justin and how they were vowed to silence while the lies were told.

"If what I was told was true, Jesus rose from the dead. That's why they say they are going home to be with Jesus. They told me I could talk to this God and he would hear me."

Jason stood up. "Marcus, I don't know what to believe. I need to go for a walk. Fresh air will do you good."

I got up and followed Jason outside. The sun felt good on my face as we walked toward the marketplace. I thought to myself, *Could there be only one God who made and knows everything and at the same time cares for me?*

I wished I could go back home and just sit in the middle of the field. I reached in my pouch for my cloth. I placed it over my face and breathed in. I knew the smell had been gone for some time now, but I still had the memory of it. If only I could… I pulled the cloth from my face. "Jason, do you smell that?"

Jason laughed. "We're in a market. I smell a lot of things."

I quickly put the cloth back in the pouch and followed my nose through the crowd. I found an old lady just closing a small bottle.

"May I?" I motioned to the bottle in her hand.

The old lady's smile turned to a scowl. "I've already paid my taxes."

I laughed. "I pay in silver."

The woman joined in the laughter. "You'll need more than silver to pay for that perfume. Your girlfriend has expensive taste."

My joy turned to sorrow. I looked down and asked softly. "Can you please just take the lid off for a moment? It was my mother's scent."

The lady motioned for me to bend down so she could speak in my ear. She whispered, "Do you have a cloth?"

I nodded, pulling the small cloth from its pouch and handing it to her.

"Do you have two silver pieces, son?"

I nodded again and produced the coins, my hand shaking.

She took the lid off and I closed my eyes and breathed in the wonderful aroma, barely hearing her words. "Be careful; this scent can be very strong."

She dipped a clear crystal into the bottle and then pulled it out and allowed the drops to fall on my cloth. It was one of the most beautiful sights I have ever seen.

"Now put your cloth away."

After I put the cloth back in its pouch she grabbed my hand and turned my palms up. Then she took the crystal and wiped it on my wrist. "Your friends may laugh, but you won't care. Your mother will be with you all day today."

The rest of the day I spent smiling.

As night fell I didn't want to go to sleep. What a day! Sighing contentedly, I closed my eyes.

Chapter 36 – Nightmare

Petula's words rang in my ears: "I saw the terror in your eyes. True strength and peace can only come from God. It comes from love, not fear."

I thought for a moment, *Didn't my mother's scent prove that?* What peace and strength I had gained from it! I sat there knowing that I must sleep and feared that I would dream. Then the old man's words came to me.

"Marcus," he said. "They are not gods at all. Tonight when they come, tell them you believe in the one true God and his son Jesus. Talk to him, Marcus. Talk to him."

What do I say? I replied in my mind. "God, I don't know what to say. Petula said true strength and peace come from you. Everything seems upside down, and I don't understand. If you are the one true God, help me to understand."

I pulled the cloth from the pouch, and the smell invaded the room. The shopkeeper was right; it was very strong. I put it back in the pouch and went to sleep.

I was once again in my nightmare. It was the same, but I was different. It was like I knew their secret. I felt excitement for the first time instead of terror. As I was being lifted I started to laugh. The higher I was lifted the more I laughed. Then everything stopped, and I heard someone say, "Enough!" I started to fall faster and faster. The old familiar laughter returned. I felt the fear coming back, and then I remembered and called out, "I believe in the one true God and his son Jesus."

Then in the blackness someone called my name.

"Marcus."

I recognized the voice, the voice of a woman.

"Marcus, ask for God's strength and peace."

As I felt the wind pushing against me I called out, "God, I need you!" Then everything stopped and I was back in the arena and Petula was standing in front of me wearing a white robe.

She smiled at me. "Marcus, may God's peace that surpasses all understanding give you strength. The world did not give you this peace, and the world cannot take it away." She smiled and then she was gone.

I closed my eyes and peace started to wash over me. I never felt like I fit in until now. I let this peace wash away all of my pain, guilt, and loneliness. I started to smell a scent, but it was not of my mother. In a moment I knew who it was. "Petula?"

"Yes."

She was standing in front of me in the barracks, her white robe shining in the darkness. "Remember the world did not give it and the world cannot take it away." She smiled a welcome-to-the-family smile and then was gone.

It was funny—I could still smell her scent. The darkness of night was being overtaken by early dawn as shadows started to form in the barracks.

Jason got up with a start. "Whew, Marcus," he whispered. "Did you leave your cloth out all night? Put it away."

I was sure I had put it back in my pouch last night. I just smiled, shook my head, and placed the cloth quickly back in my pouch. "We have both been fools, my friend."

Jason waved his arms, trying to dissipate the odor. "Yeah, me for taking you to the market and you for smelling up the place."

"No, I am talking about power. We always thought that power comes from the tip of a sword, but there is power swords cannot touch. Even death cannot touch. In fact, death only makes it stronger."

"What?" said Jason, a little louder that he intended, causing a few men to stir. "There is no power greater than death and after that the gods and torment."

"The gods are a lie, Jason. You hear me? The gods are a lie."

"Do not say such things; who knows what they will do?"

"They will do nothing. . . because they are nothing." As I said those words a power I have never felt came over me. "I believe in the one true God, and his power comes from love. His love for us."

"The gods only love themselves; they do not care about us," said Jason.

"Yeah," said Talous, the garrison commander. "They could care less about us. What's this about? Why the early morning debate, and what is that strong odor?

Talous always asked a lot of questions, not to get an answer but to stop the conversation.

"Good morning, sir," Jason said. "We were talking about nothing. Nothing at all." He eyed me as he spoke.

"You are absolutely right, Jason. We were talking about nothing." Then I could not help but smile. "The gods, nothing—same thing because the gods are…nothing."

"Marcus, careful now, son." Talous looked a little nervous as he whispered. "I may even agree with you, but you could find yourself on the wrong side of a sword with talk like that."

I unsheathed my sword and waved it in the air. "But I am on the wrong side of the sword now and have been my whole life."

Talous grabbed the handle of his sword. "A man only draws his sword for two reasons: to use it, or to clean it. I hope you intend on cleaning your sword, Marcus."

"My dear Talous, there is a third," I said as I sat on the side of my cot. "Watch." I grabbed the tip with my free hand and proceeded to break it over the top of my leg.

"To spank yourself?" said Talous amongst the peals of laughter as the sword bounced off my leg and would not break.

I took hold of the handle with both hands. "No, this!" I said as I slammed it on the stone floor, shattering it into pieces.

The laughter stopped, and there was complete silence for about a minute, followed by whispering.

Then one of the new men yelled out, "Pledge your allegiance to the garrison and to Rome, Marcus!"

I just smiled. "My whole life I have searched for power and have found it at the tip of my blade. I enjoyed watching the fear in someone's eyes as I introduced them to death. The truth is, it only helped to mask my own fear. Death will come to all of us. I have found a power stronger than this garrison, stronger than Rome, stronger than the gods, and yes, even stronger than death. Death, which I no longer fear."

At this, some men turned white like stone and others became mad, grabbing and beating me until Talous stopped them.

"Unless you want to meet with death, Marcus, I suggest you stop now! Jason, lock him up and have him scheduled for this afternoon's games."

"You went too far," Jason whispered as he led me away.

As we approached a cell of Christians who were scheduled for that day's games I asked Jason, "Do me just one last favor—schedule me with Talous."

"Sure, that way it will not be me," he said in a hollow voice. "What should I do with your things?"

"Take them to my mother. Give her a kiss for me and tell my father I found The Way. He will know what I mean."

"You are a hard man, Marcus. This is a hard thing you ask." He looked old and worn.

"Thanks, Jason. A better brother no one has ever had. I will pray for you."

As the guard locked the gate Jason turned, shook his head, and was gone.

The Christians gathered around me asking questions. Some of them were shouting and singing. I told them as much as I could in the little time I had. The elder prayed with the group that had been scheduled to go first.

I was stripped to just my loincloth and led out into the arena. I could hear some praying as I fixed my eyes on Talous and smiled.

"Marcus, why do you do this to me?" Talous said as he pointed his sword at me.

"I wanted to show you the power that is greater than death." As I said it, his sword started to shake so badly he had to grab the handle with both hands.

"Marcus!" he cried as terror filled his eyes. "I. . ."

"You need to help him, Marcus." It was Petula again, facing both of us. "Remember how I helped you?"

"Here, let me help you, my friend," I said as I grabbed the blade. "Now!" I commanded. It was strange. We were very close now. I could feel his breath and see the reflection of myself smiling in his eyes that were filled with terror. For a moment I thought he had turned the sword on himself. Then I felt the soft warm hand of Petula as I felt my body slip to the ground. The coliseum faded away, and then I was here.

Chapter 37 – Silly Place

Mathew got up and stretched. "I don't think you can ever say you don't have a story, big guy."

"None of us can," replied Rose as she twirled around and around. "And each one shows just how much God loves us."

Then she ran off with Marcus close behind.

"Where are they going?" asked Matthew.

"There's only one way to find out," Jesus said as he started to run toward Rose and Marcus.

Mathew ran with Jesus. "Where are they going?"

"To a silly place."

"A silly place?"

"Yes, a silly place."

Matthew stopped. "Here in heaven?"

"Yes, of course here in heaven. Why not?"

"Well. . ." Matthew paused. "That's not very religious."

Jesus laughed. "That's good because it's about relationships, not religions."

"What about religion? I thought that religion was important."

"Religion is man's way of putting God in a box, and God is kinda outside of the box. God is very creative, true?"

"Yeah, I guess so."

"You guess so. The heavens. . . earth . . . man . . ."

"Oh yeah. Sorry, I just don't think about God that way."

"Why?"

"I'm not sure."

"Because you have been reading a bad tabloid version of who God is instead of knowing him for yourself. Having a relationship."

Matthew looked down and thought. "Like our relationship?"

Jesus smiled. "Exactly. Much better than religion."

"So God can really be silly?"

"Oh yeah. God is very serious about being silly. Remember he created every silly bone in your body."

"I'm not ticklish."

"Sure," Jesus said as he started to run. "I think it is time for you to go to the silly place."

Matthew began running, too, and soon he was alongside Jesus. After running through the woods into a clearing that sloped down about a hundred yards they came upon a moving pool of what looked like molten liquid pearl. Children of all ages were being thrown into the air, shot into the air, and caught again by the molten liquid. The kids were screaming with delight.

"Well this is the place!" Jesus declared with one of his bigger-than-life smiles.

Matthew couldn't see any adults. "Is this place just for kids?"

"Well, kind of. . . No adult has ever made it down there."

"It does look like fun," Matthew said.

"It is. There's nothing like it. Go for it, Matthew!"

"I will," said Matthew as he stood watching.

Jesus stood there watching Matthew. "I thought marines were tough."

"Marines don't do silly well."

"Like I said, no adult has ever made it down there."

"Well I'm going to be the first," Matthew said as he started to run down the slope. "I don't care what anyone thinks, I just want to. To-oo." His voice cracked. "Have fu-un."

As he continued, he noticed his arms were smaller and slender. "Weird."

He was very close now and ran into the mass, but the mass of colorful liquid aluminum walled up, staying just out of reach, and his feet remained on the soft grass. Matthew stopped and looked at his reflection in this molten mirror that began to move to surround him. He was a kid again.

"Cool," he said as he looked at himself. He started to make funny faces. Then he touched the wall, and his finger disappeared into the warm ooze. When he removed his finger the waves rippled across the mirror, making its own funny face with Matthew's image.

He tried to touch it again, and this time it moved away from him. He would run this way and that, stop, and turn around, but it was always just a little bit faster. Sometimes when he stopped he could touch it, but he could never just run into it.

"All systems are go." The words came from nowhere as Matthew felt the ground starting to vibrate. He looked down and saw that the grass had been replaced by the ooze, and it rose and formed a tube around him. "Ten, nine, eight, seven, six," the words continued.

Matthew joined the countdown. "Five, four, three, two, one, blastoff!" he yelled as he was shot out of the tube about ten feet into the sky. The ooze caught him and twirled him inside another tube, which went back to the mirrored cylinder he started in.

"Again!" Matt said and the countdown started with Matt joining in. "Ten, nine, eight, seven, six, five, four, three, two, one, blastoff!"

This time Matt shot up into the sky forty feet and could see Jesus watching and laughing in the distance. He fell into a tube that spun around three times, but instead of slowing down, he sped up before he was shot into the air again. This time he soared one hundred feet into the sky. He could see over the treetops as he slowed and stopped for a moment, suspended in midair. Then he started to fall again. All the sensations were flooding his senses, and he wanted more.

Each time Matthew found himself back at the launch pad. When he said "more," he would be shot high through the air where he could look at the beautiful hillsides and meadows that surrounded him.

This time the ground didn't vibrate; it shook as he was shot thousands of feet in the sky. In the distance he could just make out a beautiful large building next to a sea that was calm as glass. Just the sight of it seemed to make everything stop for a moment of awe and wonderment.

This time when he fell he seemed to shoot right through the ooze and come out the bottom. With the ooze stretching all around him like a rubber band, he burst through the bottom of this molten cloud and found himself suspended over what looked like hundreds, maybe thousands of galaxies.

As he sat there suspended, a peaceful silence overtook him. "Wow, you made all this," Matt said. He felt a hand push him on this giant cosmic swing.

Swinging suspended between the molten cloud and space, Matt felt such peace. "You are my Creator," Matthew said with a Jesus smile.

Matt felt arms surround him as he was now a very young child being held in his heavenly Father's arms. Just being there made him feel. . . special. Jesus was right—it's the relationship that counts. Then he fell asleep.

Chapter 38 – Danger Zone

The clean, fresh scent of lavender drew Jane from her sleep. The smell of bacon and coffee cut through the small pockets of sleep left in her mind. Jane got out of bed and stretched. She prayed, "Lord, bless this home, this refuge in the time of my storm."

Pastor Brightwell and his wife Dolores had found out years before a wonderful way to wake up their guests. Twenty minutes before their visitors' wake-up time they would light a lavender candle and turn on a small fan facing the hallway toward the guest room. Ten minutes later they would start the coffee and bacon. It worked every time.

Dolores came upon the idea one day when she passed a restaurant that was pumping the smell of fried chicken out onto the streets. They were always packed.

This was the first real sleep Jane had had in days. After a quick shower and breakfast she jumped into her car for the five-minute drive to Memorial.

"I wonder how Daniel made out?" she asked herself as she drove.

He had insisted on staying. She only agreed when Doctor Allison stopped by to begin his twelve-hour shift. He said he would check on Daniel and show him around.

"Come on mom, Doctor Gray said Dad might be able to hear me. There's so much I want… need to say. I just need to say it, even if he can't hear me."

She knew what he meant; she had already had several late night chats with Matthew. It was hard for her to tell Daniel no, and this time she couldn't bring herself to do it. Besides, she knew he was right.

As she entered the ICU waiting room she saw Daniel sitting in the corner with Doctor Allison.

Daniel jumped to his feet. "Hi mom."

She gave him a hug as she looked at Doctor Allison. "I hope he wasn't too much of a bother."

"On the contrary, he was a pure delight."

He put his hand on Daniel's shoulder as he passed by. "See ya, Daniel. I'm going to go check on Doctor Gray. The nurse will come get you when Doctor Gray is done with his exam."

Jane smiled. "Thank you, Doctor Allison."

"Yeah, thanks," Daniel echoed.

"You're both very welcome," he said as he disappeared beyond the closing ICU doors.

"Mom," Daniel whispered. "He's a Christian!"

"I knew it. That's great Daniel."

"He said some of the doctors are going to lunch after their shift ends and we're invited."

"I don't know, Daniel. I need to spend some time with your dad."

"The trauma team's going to be there."

"You can go; just don't be gone too long, and someone will need to give you a ride back."

"Okay, but it would be better if you came."

"Daniel, I really wish I could, but I need to be with your father."

The nurse opened the ICU glass doors. "Mrs. Peterson, Doctor Gray said you can come in now."

Daniel and Jane followed the nurse through the doors.

Jane grabbed Daniel's hand and squeezed. "You understand."

Daniel gave his mom a hug. "I'll tell you all about it."

"How'd he do last night?"

"Numbers were okay, no change, but it was good to have alone time with him. It was awkward at first, but after a while I felt like he could hear me. I'm glad I stayed."

The nurse attending Matthew left his room as they were about to enter. "Hi Daniel, Mrs. Peterson. Doctor Gray will see you in a few minutes."

They both entered the room and were about to sit down next to Matthew's bed when they both stopped in horror. The numbers were in the danger zone!

Chapter 39 – Fathers House

Matt could feel the smile on his face as he started to wake. He found himself lying on a bed in the corner of a good-sized room. He felt fresh and new. If there could ever be such a feeling, he was experiencing it now. He walked to the window and looked at the garden below. He stepped back and looked at his arms and legs. "Old again," he thought to himself as he looked at the beautiful skyline. "But that's not how I feel."

"Why not?" asked an unfamiliar voice from behind him.

Matt turned around to see an older man standing in the doorway smiling. "Why not what?"

"You look at the beauty of the garden and the hills beyond and you say that's not the way you feel?" He looked at Matt with an are-you-from-Mars smile.

"Oh. . . No, that's not. . . I was looking at myself being old, and that's not how I feel."

The old man started to look at himself. "I'm old."

"Yeah. . . Ah, old is good, but it's not how I feel," Matt said as he looked down.

The old man walked in. "Hi, Matthew. I'm Eli. You can call me E."

"E."

"Yes, just E. Simple and sweet," His eyes wrinkled as he spoke. "If you are a Star Trek fan, you can call me 5 of 26."

Matt thought for a moment, then laughed. "Cute, I think I'll stick with E. How did you know my name? By the way, I prefer Matt."

"Easy. I helped set up this room for Matthew Peterson. I've just been waiting and collecting till I could meet you in person. How do you like it? Take a look around and tell me what you think?"

"That's why this place seems so familiar," Matt said as he looked around the room. First he grabbed his old baseball glove, then the football. "My books..." he said as he flipped through several Landmark books. This place is great. So many memories..."

"Excellent, I'm glad you're pleased" said E. "Gum?"

"Gum?" replied Matt as he tried on his old glove.

"Exactly, gum. Want a stick?" E asked again as he walked toward Matt.

"Sure, I'd love some," Matt said, and he took a stick from E and put it in his mouth.

"Hey Matthew, how do you like your room?" Jesus asked as he entered the room.

"It's great, and oh, you can call me Matt."

Jesus and E looked at each other. "Silly place."

"That happens a lot," Jesus continued.

"What happens a lot?" asked Matt, only half listening as he thumbed through some of the books.

"You want to change your name? Right, Scoop?"

Matt immediately recognized the voice as its owner came into the room to join the three of them. He ran to meet his sister. "Cheryl!" he exclaimed as he gave her a big hug.

"I almost didn't think you'd make it, Scoop," Cheryl said as she gave her brother a big squeeze. "Let me take a look at you." She tried not to laugh but couldn't help herself. "EEEE," she squealed.

"What?" E said. "It was his gum."

Matt looked at the three of them. "My gum? I don't have any gum."

"Oh, little brother dear. Remember my first date?"

"Your first date?"

"Yes, remember the gum that will make my mouth minty fresh."

"Minty fresh gum?" Matt swallowed his last words and tried to cover his teeth.

"Too late!" Cheryl said, as all three started to laugh at Matt and his black teeth.

Matt quickly scanned the room for a mirror or something with a reflection. He walked over to a desk on the far side of the room and picked up a picture frame. He turned it around, trying to position the glass so he could see his reflection. He could just make out his faint reflection in the glass, and for a moment his laughter joined those from the other side of the room.

Then he saw it. Through his faint reflection he saw the picture. It was the one he had on his desk at work. Even though it was a few years old it was one of his favorites, a picture of Jane, Daniel, and him at the beach.

Jane and Daniel, the two loves of his life. He stared into the picture and closed his eyes. He had been having such a great time he had forgotten what they must be going through. As he stared at their picture he sank to his knees.

Cheryl was already at his side. She put her arm around him. "Let's pray."

Matt nodded and cleared his throat, not waiting for someone else to start. He could feel Jesus and E behind him. "God, this is Matt again. I'm glad you know my heart because you know that I didn't mean to forget Jane and Daniel even for a moment. I know it was you who held me safe, and I just want that for them. I don't want what I messed up to cost them. Hold them close. I. . ." He couldn't continue.

"Lord," Cheryl continued, "thank you for loving my family even more than I did myself. Even when I thought it was hopeless, you never gave up, and now my brother is here with me."

"Go where we cannot go and do what we cannot do. Send believers to comfort and encourage. Keep them strong. Send your angels to protect them from the seen and unseen. Take the tragedy that they see and turn it for good. It is so good to have Matt here. Thanks."

Matt felt a tugging in his heart that was very strong and deep for someone he didn't even know. "God, this is Matt again." Then he started to sob. "There is this young boy. I don't even know his name, but you do. This boy is in a lot of trouble and probably doesn't have anyone to pray for him. You know the boy I'm talking about. He needs a lot of help, and he's headed to a bad place. His face looked so scared. Give him someone to care for him and help him. I just know he's sorry for what he did. I was no better than him and you saved me. Thank you for. . . I don't know where to start. It's so much and so big."

"Remember this," Cheryl said. "Jesus loves me, this I know, for the Bible tells me so. Little ones to him belong; they are weak but he is strong."

"That's me," said Matt. "A little one, and I am weak, but boy is he strong."

Matt noticed Jesus' hand on his shoulder. "Great song, Matt. Take a look in the bottom right drawer in your desk."

Matt got up, and Cheryl gave him a big hug. "Gotta go!"

"Thanks," he said, watching her disappear down the hall.

Matt reached around the desk and opened the drawer. Inside the drawer was a long, flat leather pouch that had been rolled up and tied. He took it out, placed it on the desk, and untied the leather strap.

When he had unrolled the pouch, he looked up, puzzled. "What's this?"

"I'll take it from here, son," E said to Jesus.

"Okay, Dad. You're in good hands, Matt. I'll see you later."

Matt turned to E. "He called you Dad, and you called him son."

"I'm comfortable being old and used to calling everyone son, so he calls me Dad."

"You didn't call me son?"

"That's because you wanted to me to call you Matt, son."

"Oh," Matt said, then he remembered the pouch in front of him. "Where did you get these? They're not mine."

"No they're not, but they could have been. You do know what they are, don't you?"

"Sure, a very nice set, I must say," Matt said as he took hold of one of the handles and slowly pulled the blade from its sheath. "Hey, these are like a set my grandfather had that I was never allowed to touch."

"You know, I think you're right. Wrap it back up so we can get going."

"Okay," Matt said, then slipped the blade back into its sheath and wrapped the pouch back up.

"Aren't you forgetting something, son?" E said, pointing to the leather pouch.

"I need them?"

"It would be pretty hard without them."

Matt picked them up. "What would be pretty hard?"

"You take your tools to work, don't you son?"

"My medical bag?"

"Well, you don't need a medical bag here, but you can think of that pouch there as your medical bag if you want." E said, then he walked out the room.

Matt looked once more around the room as he picked up the pouch.

"You comin'?"

Matt followed E down a small hallway and out a door that led to an outdoor fountain. They walked past the fountain and entered another door, which opened up into a large kitchen where people were busy making all kinds of food. Everything smelled wonderful.

"Don't even think it; we've got work to do. We'll get a taste later."

The front of the kitchen had a huge double door that led into a large hall that stretched as far as the eye could see. Along each side there were doors about one every hundred feet. The hall was very busy with people doing all kinds of work.

"E, what are we doing here?"

"To see your new patient, doctor."

"Cute."

E walked up to one of the large oak doors, which was lying across two saw horses. "Here he is."

Matt looked at the carving set in his hands. "Oh no. I would love to, but no. I'm just. . . well, I guess…what if I ruin the door?"

"Just give it your best. Got to go set up another room."

"Will I see you later?"

"You can count on it, son."

Everything stopped for a second as the two men faced each other and Matthew tried to get the words out. "Thanks, Dad."

E's face exploded into hundreds of wonderful wrinkles as he smiled. "You're welcome, son."

Matt watched as E walked back toward the kitchen. He almost dropped the bag as he noticed the weight in his hand. He stared at the blank piece of wood. "You know you always wanted to be creative ," he said to himself.

He closed his eyes and all kinds of shapes and designs started to fill his mind. He opened the bag and laid out his tools on the small workbench that had been set up next to the door. He picked up the sketch pad and pencil and sat down on a chair next to the door.

He rubbed his hand on the bare wood. "I'll just make a few drawings."

He closed his eyes again, and this time he started to see images of heaven and earth flashing before him like he was flipping through a card catalog. "God's love—that's what I want to show, but it's something I still don't understand."

He's Mine! Those beautiful words rang through Matt's soul as he saw himself being set free.

"That's it!" Matt said as he opened his eyes and started to draw. The more he drew, the more he was pulled into his work. He chuckled to himself that part of the scene carved in the door would be a gate.

He drew the scene from all angles: from inside heaven peering through the open gates, from outside heaven looking in, and even one from up above. Each scene showed him on his knees holding a sword on the ground with all of the ties to his old life severed. Each time he completed one of the scenes, he laid it on the door.

"I like the view from heaven best."

Matt was so into his project that he didn't even noticed E had returned and was standing by his side. "How long have you been here?"

"Long enough to enjoy watching you become submerged in your project. What do you call it?"

"He is Mine," Matt said proudly. "I think you're right; the view from heaven is special."

"I think all of the scenes are special."

They both turned to see Jesus behind them.

"It will be a hard decision," E agreed.

"Dad, okay if I pull Matt away for a little while?"

"Sure, Son. You ready for a break, Matt?"

"You can come along if you like," Jesus said.

"Yeah, E why don't you join us?"

"I'd love to, but I've got a lot to do. I'll be there in spirit though. Who knows? Maybe I'll meet up with you later."

Chapter 40 – Good News

"Where are we going?" Matt asked as he followed Jesus through the open doorway.

Jesus started down one of the paths made of gold. He stopped, looked down the path, then back up at Matt and started to chuckle. "Just follow the yellow brick road."

"I'm not from Kansas, and this definitely is not Oz."

"But this is a yellow brick road," Jesus said with a smile. "Gold, there is just nothing like it for pavement, feels great on your feet. Not too hot, not to cold, just right."

"Sounds like porridge, not pavement."

Chuckling, Matt just shook his head. "Where are we going?"

"On an adventure, Matt; you do like adventures, don't you?"

"Well, yeah," came Matt's slow response.

"You sound so excited."

"It's just I don't know what to expect."

"That's why it's called an adventure," Jesus said as they left the path and entered an area of thick forest.

Matt could hear the sound of rushing water as they made their way through the thick brush. The further they went the more wildlife they saw and heard. He saw a man standing in the clearing next to a pool of water at the base of a waterfall.

Jesus waved at the man. "Hi, Charles!"

"I knew you'd come," Charles said as he gave him a bear hug. Then he extended a hand to Matt. "Hi, I'm Charles."

"Hi, I'm Matt. Where are we?"

"New Guinea, near the Momboto tribe."

"Earth? We're on earth?"

"Well, yes. . . and no," Charles said, looking at Jesus to explain.

"Remember the church where we saw Daniel?"

"Yes. Oh, so we're here, but we are not here?"

"Not exactly. The reality is, we *are* here. They just can't see or hear us."

Charles motioned for them to follow. The three walked about a mile on a path next to the small stream that ran from the pond where they met. The path split, and Charles took the one leading away from the stream into tall grass. This path seemed to make a large half circle, meeting up with the other path again in a small clearing.

Matt saw three men in the clearing. Two looked like natives and one was a westerner. As they approached, he saw the face paint on the stocky native. He held a spear in one hand and a machete was tucked in the band around his waist. The other native was tall and thin and was standing in the middle facing the two men.

The westerner looked up into the sky. "Lord, help me to help and guide me to guide."

"Massa Andrew, do you want me to start translating?" asked the taller native.

At that moment, Charles and Jesus each put a hand on Andrew's shoulder.

"Yes, Digi, please do." Andrew looked straight at the other native. "Hi, I am Andrew, and I bring you good news."

"Mala, dingy Andrew dingy schallow da netty pit."

"What is your name?"

"Tinna er la kikkie be?" asked Digi.

"Kikkie be la Jadaus, ginka la Sheria day, oma da trara," he said, tapping the end of his spear on the ground.

"My name is Jadaus, warrior of Sheria day, on whose ground you trespass."

Andrew put his hand inside his jacket and pulled out a Bible and held it out. "I come in—"

Jadaus saw the Bible, dropped his spear, and fell face down on the path throwing dirt on this head. "Dingas ray! Dingas ray! Dingas ray!"

Andrew dropped to his knees and went to touch Jadaus.

"No, please no toucha Jadaus. Not yet."

Jadaus' chant echoed through the jungle. "Dingas ray! Dingas ray! Jadaus la Dingas ray!"

"What is he saying?"

He is saying "Undone, undone, Jadaus is undone." Over and over again.

"Digi, what did I do?"

"I don't know, Massa Andrew. Jadaus took one look at your Bible and threw himself on the ground and started chanting."

"I am going to pray for him, Digi. Would you please translate?"

"Surely."

"Dear Lord of heaven and earth."

"Donca Numia la Yarria la kinka.'

"We thank you for bringing us to Jadaus today."

"Donka kin la loopa e jac Jadaus en la pella en to."

"To tell Jadaus of your good news."

"La yaya Jadaus dingy schallow da netty pit."

At this Jadaus seemed to writhe in pain and shake his head. "No netty pit. No netty pit la Jadaus. Jadaus la Dingas ray. Jadaus la Dingas ray!"

Andrew's voice grew louder as he continued. "To tell Jadaus that you created him."

"La yaya Jadaus da schalla grupa Jadaus."

"To tell Jadaus that you love him."

"La yaya Jadaus da schalla soonia Jadaus."

Jadaus stopped his chant and looked up at Andrew for the first time after throwing himself to the ground. With his short cropped hair and face full of dust he started to weep uncontrollably, creating small streams through the dust on his face as deep sadness flowed from his words. "No soonia la Jadaus. Jadaus naharra. Jadaus naharra. No soonia la Jadaus."

Digi's tears were flowing now. "No love for Jadaus. Jadaus bad. Jadaus bad. No love for Jadaus."

Jadaus was on his knees now, frantically digging through the belt around his waist. "No soonia la Jadaus." He found what he was looking for and held it out to Andrew with shaky hands as he bowed his head. "Ya, no soonia la Jadaus. Jadaus naharra. Jadaus Dingas ray."

Digi translated as Andrew looked at a thin piece of gold. "No love for Jadaus. See, no love for Jadaus. Jadaus bad. Jadaus undone."

Andrew felt the smooth gold. It had been beaten into a thin layer and folded in toward the center on one side, like a small one-inch envelope. He opened the flaps of gold to find a small piece of paper embedded in the gold. The edges were stained red, and the only readable text was "I AM."

Matt could hear soft weeping, but it wasn't coming from Andrew or the two natives. It was Charles with his hand still on Andrew's shoulder, tears flowing freely as he looked at the piece.

Jadaus looked again and told Andrew the story of a white man that came to this spot many years ago. "This white man talked of good news and carried one of those," Jadaus said, pointing a shaking finger at Andrew's Bible. Jadaus killed the white man and ate him.

He also ate the book which had been soaked with the white man's blood. All except the small piece that he wrapped in gold. He found that piece between his victim's fingers, and to Jadaus's horror, the only thing on the paper was **IAM**. It reminded him of the symbol carved in the large stone which they worship and sacrifice to as a god. Jadaus knew that he had killed god's messenger and given him to his tribe to eat. Jadaus knew someday god would send another messenger to destroy Jadaus and his soul.

Jadaus held his machete to Andrew. "You kill Jadaus now and send his soul to be tormented."

Andrew showed the little piece of paper. "I AM is how the one true God describes himself. This book is full of words about God, about you and about me."

"It tells how Jadaus is bad and that Jadaus must die?"

"Yes, it tells how Jadaus is bad. How Andrew is bad," he said, pointing to himself. "And that even Digi is bad."

Digi nodded his head.

"You not bad like Jadaus. Jadaus must die."

"God, the I AM, says in his book that all are bad and the penalty is death."

"That is not good news. I AM must be mean."

"No, no, God loves us all and does not want any to die. He created us and loves us so much that he sent his own son to become a man like us."

"Where is he? He must be a king with all power."

"Yes, he is the King of kings but not of this world. The reason he came was to show us the way to God, the I AM, our father in heaven."

"Our father, the I AM, our Father. How can that be? What is this way?"

"God, the I AM, loved us so much that he sent his son Jesus that we all would be saved. His son was the only one without sin. God, the I AM, did not send Jesus to condemn us but that all who believe in him would be saved."

"I AM is good. He sent his son. I believe in him and want to be saved."

At that moment, Matt saw a bright light come down, enveloping the entire group.

"Now we will talk to God, the I AM. I will help you; just repeat after me: God, I know I am bad."

"God, I know I am bad," Jadaus said as the reality of his sins gripped his soul.

"I know I deserve to die."

Jadaus was openly weeping now. "I know I deserve to die."

"Please forgive me for all the wrong I have done," Andrew said through tears of his own.

"Please forgive me," Jadaus pleaded, "for all the wrong I have done."

"For without you I am undone," Andrew continued.

"For without you. . . I am undone." Jadaus broke down and wept for several minutes.

Andrew reached out and touched Jadaus on the back of the head and continued, "I believe in your son Jesus, that he came to set me free."

Digi nodded in approval as he continued the translating.

New life started to flow through Jadaus as he spoke the words that turned darkness to light. "I believe in your son Jesus. That he came to set me free."

Andrew was smiling now, a smile that could be heard in his voice. "God, I give my life to you. Come in and change my life and make it brand new."

As Digi translated, Jadaus stood up.

Then he raised his face and hands to the sky. "God, I give my life to you." He beat his chest as he continued, "Come in and change my life and make it brand new."

Matt was watching. As Jadaus held his hands up, everything seemed to stop and the heavens opened with a hush that slowly absorbed all the sound. Jesus and Charles were smiling.

"Hey Matthew."

Matt turned around, startled to see Eli standing behind him. "How long have you there? Did you see it?"

"I never miss it. Watch this," Eli said as he walked over to Jadaus.

Matt saw both Jesus and Charlie beaming with delight. Jesus pointed Matt back to Eli so he wouldn't miss it.

Eli slowly raised his right hand and stretched out a finger, gently touching the palm of Jadaus's right hand.

Then all of the sound that the hush had silenced flooded back. As the sound grew, the wind of heaven came and blew through the area. The light grew brighter and brighter and then in an instant it was gone. Eli was standing beside Matt, smiling, with a tear in his eye.

"I'm brand new. I'm brand new." Jadaus was jumping around, first grabbing Andrew, then Digi. "I AM did it! I'm brand new. I'm brand new."

"Yes he did, Jadaus. This is the good news," Andrew said, smiling.

"But how did he do it? How did he take away all of my badness?"

"Jesus paid the price for all of our sins," Andrew said, still smiling.

"How did he pay?" Jadaus asked.

Andrew tried to explain: "He paid with his blood. He died for all our sins."

"What?" Jadaus said, staring at Andrew.

"Jesus took our place."

Jadaus looked into the sky. "Take it back. Take it back." Then he fell to the ground. "Jesus no. Jesus no. Jadaus no want you to die! Jesus no. Jesus no," he cried with his face in the dirt.

Andrew's heart broke as he realized that Jadaus knew nothing of Jesus' resurrection. "Jadaus, there is more good news."

Jadaus just shook his head. "There can be no good news if Jesus is dead."

"Jadaus, Jesus' death isn't the end of the story. After being dead for three days, he rose from the dead. Jesus defeated death and the grave."

Jadaus stopped and looked up at Andrew with childlike eyes.

"He's alive, Jadaus! He's alive," Andrew said, helping Jadaus to his feet.

"Jesus, son of I AM is alive? He is really alive? I want to meet him," Jadaus said. "These are strange and wonderful things."

"Jesus has gone back up to heaven with God his father to prepare a place for each one of us. Jesus said one day he would return to take us home. Until then we have his Holy Spirit that lives inside of each one of us."

"I AM in me! I AM is in me!" Jadaus shouted over and over as he gave himself a big hug and spun around. Then he started laughing.

Before long, everyone was laughing. Jadaus slapped Andrew on the back. "We must go share this good news."

Within minutes Matt could hear the laughter of the small band fade into the brush as Andrew, Digi, and Jadaus walked toward the village. Jesus and Charles were not far behind. Jesus had his arm around Charles's neck like a coach sharing something special with his star player.

Eli looked at Matt. "I think I'm just going to rest a spell in that piece of shade by the pond. Care to join me, son?"

"Sure," Matt said and followed Eli.

Chapter 41 - Why

Eli found a large, smooth rock at the water's edge and sat down.

Matt sat down next to him and stared into the water. "There are a lot of lost people in the world, aren't there?"

"One is too many, Matt."

"Yes, that's true. Even the two young men involved in my murder…if they just could know the truth. Why can't we see it, Eli?"

"What?"

"Truth."

"Because man sees things through his pride. Truth and trust are brothers. Man wants truth as he sees it and will only trust in his hands. Just like the caterpillar who thought he would die."

"What?"

Eli's wrinkled face beamed. "I heard you like stories."

"Sure do."

Eli began.

* * *

There once was a caterpillar named Carl. He was much smarter than the other caterpillars, always knowing where the freshest, best-tasting leaves were. Most of all, he knew places that were safe.

Spring turned into summer and Carl and his friends ate, played, and soaked in the sun. When summer ended and the days and nights grew colder, Carl's friends started knitting little homes, attached to leaves and twigs, to keep them warm.

Carl tried to get them to stop, but they wouldn't. "Remember, we need to move from place to place to be safe."

They did not listen, staying warm and cozy in their new little homes all winter long.

Carl struggled all winter to find food and a new warm place every few days.

The days finally grew warmer, and Carl found his way back to his friend's homes. To his horror, all of his friend's homes had been ripped open. He looked everywhere, but none of his friends could be found. Why didn't they believe him?

Carl looked at one of the broken homes. "Move place to place so you'll be safe... God, why did you let this happen?"

Just then a beautiful butterfly swooped low and landed next to him. Even the beauty of the butterfly couldn't make him happy. "Why didn't God do something?" he asked the butterfly.

At this the butterfly got very excited and jumped on top of one of the homes and tried to tell him what happened, but Carl couldn't understand butterfly. The only word he could make out was "God."

"Did God do this?"

The butterfly softly said something Carl didn't understand, gave a sad smile, and flew away.

What a horrible thing for God to do. Carl was determined to not let this happen to other caterpillars. He would tell them of the horror and show them one of the homes his friends made that had been torn apart.

Carl and his new friends prepared all summer long for the cold winter months. When the cold came, they would have places to go.

"Remember, move place to place to be safe," they would tell each other.

That winter was hard on the caterpillars. No one dared to knit himself a warm little home for fear of what would happen. They moved place to place to be safe.

"In the spring you will see beautiful butterflies. They warned me about the danger of the little knitted homes and will be so glad to see us this spring," Carl told the others.

The sun grew warm, but the butterflies never came.

The other caterpillars asked Carl what happened to the butterflies. He thought for a long time, then the answer came to him.

"God must have been angry at the butterflies for telling me what he had done to my friends, so this year he took them."

* * *

"Sounds a lot like me, or what I was like," Matthew said.

"Matthew, remember these?" Eli said, holding out a small bag. He handed it to Matt.

Matt's face lit up. "My marbles."

Chapter 42 – Memories

Matt opened the bag, fishing for his favorite marble.

"Looking for this?" Eli said. He was holding up a large clear marble to his eye.

"That's my favorite," Matt said as he gave Eli a puppy-dog face and held out his hand.

Eli placed the crystal sphere in Matt's hand. "Remember when you got that one?"

"Yeah," Matt said as he studied the Cleary up close. As he looked through the marble, he could see the whole world. As he watched, the scene changed to a playground. The marble seemed to suck him in, transporting him to the playground to watch his younger self play marbles.

"Hey guys, want me to show you a new game?" a young man said as he approached the small group of boys.

"Sure, why not," said Matt, the leader of the group. "What you got in the bag?"

The young man looked inside. "Just some old marbles."

"Oh," said Tim, Matt's friend, paying little attention.

"Can we see?" Jimmy, Tim's younger brother, curiously inquired. Tim gave him an elbow in the ribs.

"Sure, you can all see, if you take turns," the young man said as he poured them out into his hand.

Matt noticed it right away and forgot all about being cool. "Mister, can I see that large clear one?"

"Sure," the man said. He tossed it to Matt.

Matt stared through the large marble, trying to regain his coolness. "You said you wanted to show us a new game. What's it called?"

'Well it's not really new. It's called Redemption. Ever hear of it?"

"Nope," said Tim. "How do you play it?"

"Redemption, that's what it's all about, isn't it?" Matthew asked as he watched the boys play.

Eli put his hand on the man teaching the boys. He turned his head toward Matthew and smiled. It was his Guardian, Raah.

Matthew smiled. "That was my favorite game. It was also one of the best summers of my life. I spent it with my Grandma. She took me to church, and I liked it. I learned a lot of the songs and even went forward once when my friends did and recited a prayer."

"What happened, Matthew?"

"I don't know if it was because summer was over or because my parents' divorce was finalized. I had to go back home, whatever *that* was. Mom and Dad tried, but things were never the same. I prayed really hard that summer, but they still got divorced; that's when I stopped a lot of things. My dad said to throw the marbles away because I wasn't a kid anymore."

"That's sad."

"What?"

"That you lost your childhood and faith because of what the world calls a 'man.' Matthew, do you remember Daniel?"

"Do I remember Daniel? Forgetting Daniel would be like forgetting my own right arm and as painful as losing it. Now *there* was a real man."

"You didn't think much of me when I left," Daniel's voice suddenly responded. The words faded before Matthew could respond as he started reliving the nightmare once again.

Daniel and Matthew were together in the all-too-familiar foxhole. As medics it was their job to get and tend the wounded. They had just waited through a shortie, which was a favorite of the Vietcong. A small group would appear from nowhere, shoot off a few dozen rounds each, and disappear into one of their famous network of tunnels.

One of the men in a foxhole in front of them had been hit. Once the all clear had been given, one of them would go to him. They had devised the "Rock, Paper, Scissors" method of deciding who would be the first to go.

"ALL CLEAR!" rang out, shattering the sounds of the early morning and putting a knot in Matthew's stomach.

"One, two, three," they said in unison.

"Paper," Matthew yelled out to Daniel's rock. Matthew started to smother Daniel's rock, but Daniel punched through Matthew's paper, shouting, "The Solid Rock breaks every chain!"

Before Matthew could make a move Daniel had grabbed his pack and started out of the foxhole. Matthew yelled "Nooo youuu dooon't," masking the sound of a single shot as everything shifted to slow motion. He saw his hand reach for Daniel, for the thousandth time, to grab his utility belt to pull him back. Time shifted back into regular speed as Daniel fell back into the foxhole.

"Hey Daniel, I didn't pull back that hard. Besides, I won fair and. . ." his words drifted off as he noticed the glassy stare and the small hole in Daniel's forehead.

"NOOO!" Matthew knew he was yelling uncontrollably, but he couldn't hear anything. He put his arms around Daniel and held him close. His hand brushed Daniel's hair back and caught on a fragment on the back of Daniel's head. Sound rushed back as Matthew withdrew his hand and saw Daniel's blood on it.

"Sniper in the top," the sound echoed through the valley.

Matthew snapped. He grabbed his automatic, jumped out of the foxhole, and yelled as he shot at the treetops. Somehow, he shot the sniper.

"Matthew," it was Eli's voice.

Matthew turned around to see Daniel standing next to Eli with the foxhole behind them.

"Daniel, how could you leave me? You know that should have been me," he said as he pointed to what was Daniel's empty shell.

"This was an answer to Daniel's prayer," Eli continued. "He didn't want you die here, not knowing where you were headed."

Matthew looked into Daniel's eyes. "You were the only one keeping me sane, with your corny jokes and assuring smile. After you left, I was alone, hurt, and angry at the God you loved so much.

Daniel put his arm around Matthew. "It doesn't matter, in the long run, that you were alone and hurt. A lifetime wasn't long enough for our friendship. I didn't want to enter eternity just to find out that you didn't make it. Do you think the accuser, deceiver, and hater of all mankind will allow friendships? What matters is where you end up."

As they both looked at Daniel's lifeless body, Daniel looked at Matthew with tears in his eyes. "I was willing to risk you being hurt and angry. I wanted you to have another chance not to become part of the walking wounded."

Matthew swallowed hard. "How many people sacrificed for me?"

Eli looked into Matthew's eyes and smiled. "As many as it took. Some in little ways and some in big ways, but all of them were beautiful."

Matthew looked down. "That doesn't say much for me."

Daniel gave him a shove. "What do you mean? Look at your son."

Matthew shuffled his feet. "Yeah, he's a great kid. Not much thanks to me."

"What about that great name you gave him?" Daniel said with a grin.

Chapter 43 – Daniel

The scene changed to a mountain-top lake in the Sierras. Eli was looking out over the lake. He was outfitted with hiking gear, complete with backpack, hiking boots, and fishing pole. He turned to Matthew. "Why did you name your son Daniel?"

"I wanted my son to be like him." He nodded to Daniel, who was still with them. "He was the truest friend and greatest man I ever knew."

Eli took off the backpack and laid it down on the small grassy beach. "Those things are heavy. Is that why you encouraged your wife to take him to church?"

"I guess I wanted him to be a better man than his father. Then later I grew to resent it. I tried to reconnect but never seemed . . . able, I guess. When he was young we did a lot together, but somehow we grew apart."

"What about this place? Eli said.

"Yeah," Matthew said sadly. "Kennedy Lake, scene of my last disaster. I wanted to do something special for his sixteenth birthday. He had always heard about my backpacking trips in the Sierras and wanted to go. I tried to plan everything right, but it seemed I did everything wrong."

"You look back through the distorted eyes of your expectations instead of the wonder of the moment. This is not a place for words but experiences. Look over there." Eli pointed down the shoreline to where a large stream fed the small lake. As he did, instantly the three of them were there.

Matthew watched in awe as he saw himself place two small grasshoppers on a hook for his son. Daniel cast into the current, which carried the small bobber and bait into the lake.

Daniel squinted at the sun's reflection on the lake. "I can't see the bobber."

A moment later his pole started to bend wildly. "I got one! I got one!" Daniel yelled as he started to reel the fish and backed away from the shore.

"Careful, he'll get off," Matthew said, lunging toward the catch. "No, you hooked him real good."

"He's not going to die, is he?"

"Nah, he didn't swallow it; just caught him in the tough part of the jaw. See?" Matthew said, pulling the hook free. "Still have one of the grasshoppers left. Daniel, I think he's a golden. Big one, too.

"Hold him like this. Put one hand under his body and tail and with your other hand put your thumb in his mouth and a finger in his gill. I didn't have time to film you catching him," Matthew said as he handed the fish to Daniel.

Matthew proudly started to film Daniel and his prize. "I really think he's a golden trout."

"He's my first one, dad," Daniel said, beaming.

"Your first fish is a large golden trout! All the years I came up to these mountains, no one has caught one. I always heard stories that they were up here. Now you have a great story of your own."

"We don't have to eat him, do we?"

"He's your fish. Maybe a beauty like this deserves to swim another day."

"Is he okay?"

"Oh yeah. Just gently place him in the water with both hands and open your finger and thumb."

Matthew filmed Daniel releasing the golden, and like a flash, he was gone.

Daniel turned toward his dad. "Wow, did you see that?"

"Yeah, got it all right here," Matthew said, tapping the side of the video camera. "I just wish I was ready when you caught him. . ."

The scene stopped, freezing Matthew in mid-sentence.

"No problem," said Eli as he pretended to be a camera man rolling the film backward. He made a counter-clockwise motion with his right hand and seemed to hold an invisible camera with his left. "Da da da da da da da da."

"What are you doing, Eli?" questioned Matthew as he and his friend Daniel exploded in laughter.

Daniel gave him a punch. "He's rewinding your film. You know, the one you didn't record."

Sure enough, Eli had rewound the scene to where Matthew was removing the hook from the fish's mouth.

"That's great, Eli. Do it some more."

Eli looked at Matthew with a pouty face. "You didn't think my da da da da was very good."

"No Eli, you were great. I would just do it differently, not better."

"Well then, let's see you do it."

"You da' man, Matthew!" cried Daniel through the tears. "Show Eli how it's done."

"I don't know how."

"Sure you do," replied both Eli and Daniel.

"Ok, here goes." Matthew started making the motion with his hands but nothing happened.

"You've got to make the sound or it won't work," Eli blurted out, trying not to laugh.

"Okay, here goes," Matthew said as he started to make the motions. "Ta th th yup york wap si dup."

"What's that?" cried Eli and Daniel in unison, their stomachs hurting from the laughter.

Matthew didn't care; it was working, and he "yup york wap si duped" in delight back to where he was putting the small grasshoppers on the hook.

He stopped with a puzzled look. "How do I get it going?"

"Say roll'em, and point your finger," said Eli with delight.

Matthew shook his head. "Are you both enjoying yourselves?"

They both nodded like two young schoolboys with the giggles. Eli pointed his finger and mouthed the words.

"I know," Matthew said as he positioned himself in front of his son. He paused a minute as he watched what he had missed before.

He could see the wonderment in his son's eyes as he watched his father bait the hook.

Matthew slowly pointed his finger. "Roll'em," he whispered, and the scene unfolded before him. He watched, rewound, watched, rewound; he watched his son catch his first fish a dozen times. He tried "freeze frame and advance," mastering pause and slow motion.

Finally Matthew turned toward Eli and Daniel, who were skipping rocks. "Talk about home movies!"

"Just like being there," Daniel said with a smile. "I think you did a great job with Daniel, Matt."

Matthew smiled. "Thanks. That means a lot coming from you."

Matthew walked back over to where his son was frozen in time. "God help him to be strong. Help him to overcome my mistakes. Continue your work in his life so he will touch others with your love."

Matthew looked across the lake and saw Rose waving to him.

Matthew glanced back at Eli.

Eli smiled. "Go ahead."

"You don't mind?"

"Not at all, son."

At that, Matthew made his way around the lake to Rose.

"Hey, Dad."

The words caused Matthew to pause, letting the words warm his soul.

"How's my beautiful Rose?"

Rose got up from the bench she was sitting on and gave him a hug.

"Great. I heard you like stories."

"Sure. I loved your telling of the Garden."

"Thanks. Now I want to tell you the story of *When Heaven Was Silent*. You celebrate it as Christmas."

Matthew leaned in as Rose began. "Eli was walking through a meadow next to a pond. He didn't seem to notice Jesus coming across the meadow toward him. Eli stopped as Jesus caught up to him at the edge of the pond, and they both stared into the water."

As Rose was speaking the mountain lake in front of them changed to a small pond on the edge of a meadow bordered by dense woods on both sides. Matthew and Rose were facing them about fifty feet away across the water, and they could see and hear everything. The silence wasn't at all uncomfortable. Instead, it drew them in deeper and deeper. After a while Matthew started seeing images in the pond. He noticed a scene from the garden with the serpent, as he watched the water stirred and the scene changed to animals of all kinds entering a giant boat. The water was disturbed again and he saw Moses throw down his staff in front of Pharaoh and it turned into a serpent. The next time he saw water parting in a large sea, and soldiers riding through it at the water came crashing down.

Matthew glanced up and noticed tears flowing down Eli's face as Jesus placed his arm on his shoulder.

Jesus spoke softly to Eli, all the while looking at the waters. "Dad, I know many of them won't understand."

"The soldiers are my children, too. Maybe I shouldn't have given them freewill."

"Then they wouldn't be children. They wouldn't be able to create. They wouldn't explore, and grow. They couldn't be like you."

"But they corrupt it and try to corrupt others."

"True. That is why we have to show them the truth."

The reflections in the waters fade and silence falls like a blanket over the meadow.

Eli's face draws you in… As you watch his mouth forms the words. "I know."

Jesus turns to face Eli. "They are ready."

"I know." Tears are now flowing down Eli's face.

"It will be but a moment."

This time Eli's voice cracks. "I know." Carreen is now by his side, rubbing his left shoulder.

Jesus puts his hand on his knees and takes a breath. "I'm feeling them."

Eli places his hand on Jesus' head. "I will be with you."

Jesus takes another breath. "I know."

With each breath Jesus was getting younger.

Eli kneels to keep at eye level with Jesus. "I will have to turn away."

At this the young Jesus jumps into Eli's arms. "I know," he whispers into his ear.

"Son, show your brothers and sisters the way home."

"I will, Abba."

"I know."

"I Love you, Daddy."

Now Eli is cradling the baby Jesus. "I Love you, son." Then Eli holds Jesus high above him and calls out for all of heaven to hear, "His name will be Jesus, for he will redeem all of mankind." Then he kisses him and hands him to Carreen.

There is complete and utter silence as Carreen walks through the meadow into a gray fog carrying baby Jesus. Matthew noticed the waters stirring again and sees the young boy that was there, in the garage, when he was stabbed.

Sound floods back as Matthew fell to his knees. "Thank you, Eli. You didn't have to, but you did."

Matthew got up, looked around, and noticed that Eli was sitting next to Rose on the bench. "Eli, I keep seeing the boy's face full of terror as he looked down on me before I passed out."

Eli looked out over the pond. "You very good at skipping rocks?"

"Not bad, I guess."

"Here's a good one," Eli said as he tossed a smooth flat stone to Matthew. "Let's see what you can do."

Matthew looked over the stone to find the best fit between his index finger and thumb. He crouched down next to the edge of the water and let it fly. It skipped along the surface across the pond before finally disappearing below the surface.

"Not bad."

"Not bad! That stone skipped too many times to count."

"Just like life, the stone disappears too quickly. But the ripples multiply, touch each other, and cover the pond; one life touches another which touches another. The young man's name is Miguel."

Matthew stared at the ripples. "I want to, need to, pray for Miguel."

Eli smiled. "Go ahead, son.'

"God, this is Matthew again. I wish I had a better way of starting, but I'm still new at this. There is this young man; his name is Miguel, and most, if not all of the lives that have touched his have been bad. He needs someone from you to touch his life. Who's going to tell him the truth? Who is going to tell him the good news?

"So many people don't know; they just don't know. They are blind to the truth, the truth of your love. You sent so many people in my path. Please send someone to Miguel so that he will know. Oh God, so many don't know. None of us are good enough. The deceiver knows that our lives, no matter how good they seem, in the end will condemn us to hell. Our only hope is in you … only in you."

Matthew started to moan as he felt the weight of the lost. He saw Miguel's face, and then he saw the walking wounded and started to feel their pain. Not just their physical pain, but their emotional pain as well.

Chapter 44 – We Don't Deserve Nothin!

"Daniel okay? He didn't seem himself when he passed the nurse's station. He looked pretty upset," Terri said as she entered Matthew's room.

Jane was in her chair next to Matthew's bed. "The high numbers hit too close to home. It made the seriousness of Matthew's condition all too real."

"I'm sorry. I should have stayed."

"It's not your fault. We just didn't know the numbers jump up for a few minutes after a vigorous exam. After Doctor Gray came the numbers went right down, just as he said they would. It's just…" Jane looked sad as she pushed the words out. "Doctor Gray said we should start thinking in terms of weeks and months. Not hours and days."

Terri placed her chair next to Jane's. "That's a hard transition to make, I know. The doctors are hopeful that it could be any day, but they need to prepare you in the event it isn't."

"Dr. Gray said he could be wrong."

"Usually they are happy when they are wrong in these cases. Doctor Gray just wants you to be prepared."

"I know, but I worry about Daniel. Reality hit him real hard."

* * *

Daniel saw that the hospital chapel was empty, so he walked past the front pew, up to the altar, and let it all out.

"Why, God? Why did you let this happen to my dad? Doctor Allison says to have faith. Well I've had faith ever since I can remember, and what happens? Nothing. Dad still doesn't know you and any moment he could slip away... right into hell. Why can you do so much for everyone else, but not my dad?"

Daniel shook his fist at the altar. "Why don't you answer?"

"Why you talkin' to God that way? God is good. We don't deserve nothin'. We do the bad stuff, not him. We don't deserve nothin'."

A small boy ran out of the shadows at the end of the front pew and pushed the much larger Daniel. "Don't you talk to God like that!"

Daniel scrunched up his nose. "Sorry."

"Why you talkin' to God like that?"

"My dad got hurt real bad."

The young boy put his hands in his jean jacket. "He gonna make it?"

"Don't know."

"Sorry."

"Yeah, why you here?"

"I messed up real bad."

"You look okay."

"I'm okay, but my heart hurts a lot. Because of me, someone got real messed up. If he dies, I know God will kill me."

"What?"

"He may kill me anyways. I don't blame him."

"God loves you."

The young boy looked Daniel square in the eye. "Don't you go makin' fun of me."

Daniel sat down in the front pew. His voice was so low the young boy barely heard him. "I'm not... God loves all of us."

The boy sat next to Daniel and stared up at the cross. "I don't think so. I'm just so much trash."

"No you're not."

"Yeah I am. That's even what my brothers call me. S. M. Trash."

"S. M?"

"So Much."

"That's mean."

"Makin' me do bad things, that's what's mean."

"God doesn't think of you that way."

His soft brown eyes met Daniel's. "It's okay. I deserve it."

"You're right, there. We all deserve it… but God wants to help us."

"Yeah, is that why you were yellin' at him?"

"I know, but he still understands me even when I'm mad or… afraid."

"I get afraid a lot."

"What are you afraid of?"

"Right now?"

"Yeah."

"God."

"Why are you afraid of God?"

"Eye for an eye, tooth for a tooth. I really messed up, and God's going to pay me back."

"One thing I'm sure of is God loves us, even when we mess up."

"Yeah, then why doesn't he answer our prayers?"

"I don't know, but he does love us."

"Stop saying that. You don't know nothin."

Daniel reached behind the pew and found a Bible in the pocket attached to the back of the pew. He held it out. "That's what God's word says."

"Where?"

Daniel opened it up to John and read about God's love. He read story after story about Jesus. How he loved the unlovely, the people this world threw away as trash, restoring them to life. He ended with Jesus asking the father to forgive us, even as he was dying on the cross, taking our place.

Chapter 45 – Cood Mews

As Matthew continued to pray he felt Eli's arms absorbing his pain. "God, help them!" he cried out and felt his body shake with their pain.

His whole body felt clammy and smelly like an old wet suit that didn't fit. For the first time since being in heaven, he felt cold. He opened his eyes. He was lying down on the rock next to the pond, unable to move. Eli was kneeling over him. He tried to speak but couldn't. Something was stuck in his mouth, hurting his throat. He couldn't move his head, arms, or legs.

He looked up into Eli's eyes, drawing himself into them for a moment as everything… stopped.

Eli smiled an I'm-proud-of-you-son smile. Matthew smiled back with an I-love-you-dad smile. Then Eli took his index finger and touched it to the palm of Matthew's hand.

What Matthew felt with that one lone touch, for one brief moment, was indescribable. It was at a level so beyond anything he had already experienced. He could see the full spectrum of light with seven primary colors and hear their sounds. He felt a love and compassion that couldn't be explained. He knew that he knew that he knew he had felt the touch of God. He was asked to ask the questions and was amazed by the simplicity and clarity of the answers.

Eli gave Matthew a smile as everything started to fade from Matthew's view. The light lost most of its color and turned from warm and inviting to cold and blinding as he closed his eyes. Again he tried to talk but couldn't. He felt so uncomfortable and struggled to move, yet the only things that would move were his fingers, and that took all the energy he had.

Matthew started hearing sounds of yelling coming through a distant tunnel. Then stillness followed with the sweet soothing voice of his wife, Jane, calling his name. He listened, realizing that he was surrounded by her scent. He smiled at the thought of Marcus and his cloth.

* * *

"Matthew! Oh my... Matthew!" Jane jumped up from her reading. "Someone get Daniel! He moved his fingers! He moved his fingers!"

Nurses and the ICU attendant came rushing in, her son Daniel close behind.

"I hear you have some good news to share," smiled the young attendant as he stood on the other side of the hospital bed.

Daniel rushed through the crowd to his mom's side.

"I was sitting reading to him. I glanced up and saw his fingers move." Focusing on Matthew, she encouraged, "Come on honey, move your fingers for me."

Everyone stared at the fingers that had not moved for three days. Ever so slowly one finger tapped twice. "There, did you see them? Did you see them?" Jane's voice raised an octave in the excitement, and the room burst alive.

Daniel grabbed his dad's arm. "It's Daniel, dad. You're in Memorial Hospital. You've been hurt, but you are going to be okay."

"We all love you," Jane added. "You've been in a coma for three days."

The attendant leaned over the bed and whispered to Jane. "You're doing great. Ask Matthew to try and open his eyes."

"Honey, it's Jane. Can you open your eyes for me?"

Matthew was now in a straight jacket that was his body. He had to work with all his might to force his eyes to let in the harsh blinding light. Through red swollen eyes, he saw Jane and Daniel. "Jaaa..nnn," he tried to speak as his body moved against the restraints.

"Shhh... honey." Jane touched his face with the side of her hand. "You have a respirator tube in your throat. You can't talk yet."

With "I love you's" in his eyes, Matthew started to cry.

Daniel worked his way around the bed, past the attendant. "It's okay, Dad; it's Daniel. We've been praying for you."

Matthew wanted to explain and move, but he couldn't do either.

"Dad, you're going to be okay, but you can't move right now."

"Don't upset him, Daniel."

At this, Matthew stopped and looked at Jane, trying to speak with his eyes. As their eyes met, he smiled. "It's okay, I love you," Jane said. Then Matthew looked at his hand.

As Jane followed Matthew's eyes to his right hand, he signed, "I love you."

"I love you too," Jane whispered through her tears as she signed the words.

Matthew looked at his dejected son and did something that had always been known but never said. He signed "I" and relaxed his throat to let the word out. "Aaa..I." Then he signed "love." Took another breath and relaxed. "Lud..va." Tears were flowing all over the room now as a small group watched in awe as Matthew pressed on, signing "you" and working to get out the words to wash over his son: "uuuu... sa san.."

Daniel's tears mingled with his father's as their foreheads met. "I love you too, Dad," Daniel whispered.

Matthew smiled and tried to sign again: T-H-A-N-K-S F-O-R T-H-E P-R-A-Y-E-R-S.

Daniel smiled and threw his arms around his dad.

Matthew's right hand started moving again.

"Ma'am, I think he wants something," said a tall handsome orderly that had entered the room.

Jane looked down at his hand, and sure enough he was signing B-I-B-L-E.

"Bible? Why are you signing Bible?"

B-I-B-L-E, he signed again.

"I can help with that ma'am," the orderly said as he walked over to the nightstand. "The Gideons put Bibles in almost every room. Here it is... hmm... it doesn't look like one of theirs," he said, handing it to Jane.

He looked directly into Matthew's eyes with a "surprise!" grin.

Matthew did a double take. It was Raah, his Guardian. He gave him a Thanks-big-guy smile with his eyes.

Jane looked puzzled. "Daniel, didn't you give your father a Bible like this last year? This one is pretty worn and marked up, though."

"Let me see it," Daniel said, taking the Bible in his hands. His hands started to tremble as he opened up to the dedication page, his lips forming the words with no sound. "From Daniel to Dr. Matthew Peterson." He turned to his dad with hurt in his eyes. "I don't get it. What's this doing here? You didn't give it away, did you?"

Matthew was frantically trying to sign "no, mine," but everyone's eyes were on Daniel.

"Daniel, we don't know that."

"But it's so marked up, Mom. How else did it get here?"

Matthew closed his eyes, not knowing what else to do. *Father, help. I don't know what to do. It's so hard here; it's so hard.*

"May I see it?" the orderly asked.

Daniel placed the Bible in the orderly's huge hand. "Sure, everyone else has."

The orderly looked at the back of the book. "Mystery solved!"

"What?" Daniel and his mom said in unison.

"See," he said, holding open the back page, which was stained dark red through some of the maps. "I heard that his briefcase was ruined, but they must have salvaged his Bible and put it in his room."

Daniel took the Bible back and started thumbing through the pages. Turning it sideways he read from the margins. Fall and Deception of Man. He flipped through a few more. Nature's Song. "Mom, he has Exodus 3:14 highlighted. 'I AM has sent me to you.' That doesn't make any sense. What is all of this, dad?"

"May I?" Jane asked with an outstretched hand.

Daniel placed the Bible in his mom's hands. "I don't understand, Mom."

She looked at some of the writing, then shook her head and smiled at Matthew. "What have you been up to, mister?"

She said to Daniel, "It's your father's handwriting, all right. Story of I Am and missionaries Charlie and Thomas. Healing of the Leper and the Parable of the Mask. Daniel, have you ever heard of the Parable of the Mask?"

"Parable of the Mask? No, not that I know of. This is really strange, mom."

Matthew was still trying to sign, but all of his energy was gone.

Daniel looked up at his dad and noticed that he was still trying to sign. "Mom, can you make that out?"

"C-O-O-D M-E-W-S. Cood mews," she said as she covered his hands with hers. "There will be plenty of time for you to tell us about your cood mews dear. Now it's time for you to rest. Welcome home."

* * *

Home—it seemed so far away now...fading through Matthew's consciousness, a verse came to mind: "For me to live is Christ and to die. . ."

The room seemed to fade. A bright light approached from the corner of the room as Carreen moved toward Matthew. A wave of peace flowed over him when Carreen touched his face. "Sleep now, young Matthew. Rest, for you are now among the living."

1 Cor 13:12

For now we see through a glass, darkly; but then face to face: now I know in part; but then shall I know even as also I am known.

(KJV)

Sojourner

I must leave
Home
       Where I belong
       Where life began.

To help other lost souls find the Way
Home
       Where they belong
       Where life is.

My heart leaps when another Sojourner I meet we talk about
Home
       Where we belong
       Where life is.

About those who have completed their journey and are
Home
       Where we belong
       Where life is.

Why are we still here you ask? To help you find The Way
Home
       Where you belong
       Where life is.

So we Sojourn Until we are called
Home
       Where we belong
       Where life is.